PRIMED TO KILL

EMMY ELLIS

CHAPTER ONE

Oliver took a deep breath. The call from a dead male to get him to the warehouse had been the first time he'd been contacted in months. He'd been nostalgic from lack of chatter from spirits, even though it took him to their death sites and he saw things most people couldn't even imagine seeing. All his life—as far back as he could remember anyway—he'd heard them, been called a weirdo by his parents, leaving home when the family taunts had finally got to be too much. He'd made it work for him, though, assisting the police on cases, coppers finally accepting he wasn't involved in the murders, that he really did hear ghosts.

The air was hot. Like someone had a bonfire going, a huge, raging one, relentless heat coming off it, enough to sear your eyebrows.

Oliver glanced around, past the police strolling the vicinity with their diligent, looking-for-clues paces. He eyed SOCO doing their thing in bootied feet and white suits, their hands covered in creamy latex. He didn't see any reason for the heat, though. No fires mounted on the walls, their orange-bar stripes belting out warmth, the image reminding him of the electric fire in the living room of his childhood. No newfangled halogens, rectangles of bright yellowy-orange that not only served as heaters but damn good sources of light that hurt the eyes if you stared at them too long.

Sweat dribbled down his back, spreading out over his armpits. He lifted his arms, put his hands on his hips casually, wondering, then not caring whether he had wet patches on his T-shirt. That kind of thing didn't matter in situations like this. The small stuff paled into insignificance by death. The everyday worries of how good you looked and whether your hair needed washing didn't figure for those called out to deal with the aftermath of some nutter's handiwork.

He stared at the corpse. Young bloke in his twenties. Christ, what a waste. He'd only just begun living really, possibly leaving home, branching out on his own. Did his parents even know where he was? How he'd ended up? Oliver imagined them going about their day-to-day business, thinking their son was at work maybe, when in reality...

He didn't envy whoever had to tell that their baby wasn't coming back.

This man would've been considered handsome in life, he reckoned. In death, though, he didn't look so good, but then who did? Even those who passed in their sleep—nothing untoward going on here, folks, move along, please—tended to bloat, their orifices oozing fluid if their body hadn't been discovered in time for Hank, the ME, to do his thing.

Oliver had had the pleasure of meeting him a few months back. Pleasure seemed such an odd word given the circumstances, but Hank was a jolly man, probably having to be so because of the horrors he saw day in, day out. Hank would determine how this man had died, because although it seemed pretty obvious strangulation was the cause—*the chain, look how tight that fucking chain is around his neck!*—it might not be so cut and dried. He could have been killed first then strung up. This was a murder, not a suicide. What the hell went through a killer's mind? Did they sit at home envisaging what they'd do to their victims? Write notes on the subject?

If he'd been told years ago he'd be standing in front of some poor, dead bastards on a regular basis, he'd have shit himself.

Funny how things turned out.

The last case had been a bad one, a first for Oliver in that he'd trailed DI Langham around to every lead, had seen each dead body as they'd piled up, and really understood the hard work that went into catching wankers who had a mind to kill. An eye-opener. Yeah, the Sugar Strands case had been that all right, and now, here he was, in a warehouse with a corpse. And this corpse, well, it was something that could be seen all over the world at any given time, someone supposedly hanging themselves. Shit that appeared on the news and internet on a regular basis—so much so that, horribly, it failed to have a massive impact. Many people saw the same thing over and over too much and got used to it.

From what he'd learnt from Langham, most people shot or stabbed their victims, a strangulation here or there, but with Sugar Strands, the victims had been mutilated, arms and legs cut off, faces peeled back, stomachs sliced open, their innards ripped out. It had been evil, no doubt about it, but this body here? It was the usual, the norm.

Regardless, this was someone's son, brother, nephew. Maybe even some kid's dad. Shit. That thought didn't sit well. He couldn't imagine being that young and trying to understand why Daddy wasn't going to walk through the front door. Why

Mummy was crying and couldn't stop. Why Daddy had even been hurt in the first place.

But the victim might not have been a particularly nice man. Hung out with mean people. Got himself into this mess. Not that Oliver thought he'd deserved it if he *had* run in the wrong circles, but most people didn't just end up this way.

There wasn't any blood, wasn't much for him to chuck his guts up about, but it was the stillness that bothered him. The whole place—from its crummy, breeze-block walls to its rough concrete floor, to its metal-girder ceiling to its dirty, age-speckled windows—held a sense of desolation mixed with foreboding that told him this wasn't just a one-off.

There would be more like this.

He sensed this as the first of many and didn't know how he knew it either. The dead hadn't told him, hadn't spelt it out, and he acknowledged that with Sugar Strands he'd evolved somehow, grown an extra sense. That was all very well, but he'd never claimed to be psychic, to know the future and the past, and now it seemed he might well be capable of that. He'd explained to those at the station that he didn't know anything until the dead told him, and they'd had to be content with that.

With Sugar Strands he'd felt different, had been able to know when something wasn't right long before they'd seen it wasn't. Small things, like seeing flashes of what lay behind a closed door or getting the feeling that something wasn't right in a certain house. But having a sixth, seventh, or fucking eighth sense wouldn't aid him in helping solve crimes quicker. Knowing something was 'off' before he entered a room wouldn't catch the killer. It just meant he felt funny, knew a little more than he had before. Had some kind of warning as to what they were walking into.

Like now. Death number one.

Around a ten-inch-wide stretch of rusty, peeling, red-painted metal went from floor to ceiling, seeming like it'd grown right out of the concrete and exited through the roof. He imagined the top of it poking into the sky, a modern-day chimney, then blinked to clear the image. He should be concentrating, waiting for the spirit to speak to him again, not allowing his mind to roam.

"You got anything yet?" Langham asked quietly.

His appearance at Oliver's side had him jumping, and Oliver shook his head, turning to study Langham for signs of stress—or the alcohol they'd consumed before coming out. Earlier, they'd got rat-arsed on wine with dinner in a nice Italian restaurant, a celebration at the end of the Sugar Strands case.

"The corpse's spirit hasn't spoken since we got here," Oliver said. "But I... This isn't..." He sighed. "This is the first of many."

"And you know this how?" Langham frowned, glancing at the body then back at Oliver. "If he hasn't spoken..."

"That feeling shit I got last time."

"Ah. Well, let's hope not, eh?" Langham ran a hand through his hair. "Last thing we need is another serial."

"Yeah."

Langham walked off, to the warehouse doorway, staring out into the night as though the darkness would give him answers. Only time would tell, obviously, whether Oliver's intuition was right, that they'd be called out to another sight like this one. It meant a second death to prove he could rely on these new feelings, so he hoped he was wrong.

He gave the body his attention again. It had been attached to the floor-to-ceiling metal, a chain looped around and around the torso up to the armpits so he was held there, feet off the floor. It made the pelvis level with an average man's face, and Oliver got a flash of information—*sex crime*—and he staggered backwards. Had this man been trussed up and used by his killer in *that* way? Oliver's ears buzzed. He was right, but damned if he knew how he was certain. He waited for more information, closing his eyes and concentrating, freeing his mind and opening himself up for data to come in.

"There's loads of them."

The spirit's voice startled him, and he snapped his eyes open, gaze meeting that of the bulbous-eyed victim.

"Loads of them?" he whispered, stepping forward. "People?"

"Yes. They...did things to me."

7

"What kind of things?" Adrenaline popped out of wherever the hell it resided inside him when it wasn't needed and spread in a head-lightening streak to every part of Oliver. He swayed, equilibrium shot, and sucked in a deep breath.

"They made me...do things."

"Go on."

"It's something they'd planned, something they've dreamt about for a long time. I'm the first."

"Shit, so I was right." Oliver gained no satisfaction in that. "Who are they?" It was a long shot, but he had to try.

"I don't know."

Oliver stifled a sigh. He hadn't expected any other answer.

"They're bald."

"Right. How many killers are there?"

"About twenty? Maybe more. I didn't...didn't... It wasn't the kind of situation where I could sit and count them."

"So what did they do?"

"They hummed."

"Pardon?"

"And swayed."

"Um..." Oliver wasn't sure what to ask next. The image of twenty or more people swaying and humming in here while this poor fucker was chained up had his blood running cold. He shook his head to clear it. "Do you know why they did this?"

"I was the one they wanted."

"Because?"

"Because I'm gay."

"Aw, fuck." Was this a gay-hater killing? Was that it?

"It was just...fun for them. A ritual they wanted to play out. They... It's getting difficult to stay here. I'm being pulled back..."

"Wait!" Oliver shouted. Panic gripped him, chasing the adrenaline around until he felt sick. He swallowed and closed his eyes. "Just hang on for a while longer. Ritual? What do you mean? Like a sex ring? What?"

Silence.

"You had him?" Langham called.

The warehouse was quiet, as if all officers had ceased work to stare at Oliver talking to the dead man. Most of them were used to it, but he'd seen a couple of new faces tonight, people who would wonder what the fuck was going on with the skinny bloke talking to himself.

Oliver opened his eyes. Langham stood beside him.

"Yes, I had him, and I was right. This is only the beginning."

CHAPTER TWO

TWO MONTHS LATER

Adam kicked at the loose stones beneath his feet. Waiting around outside the mini-mart down the road from the flat he shared with his brother wasn't his idea of a good time, especially when Dane was late finishing and the rain pissed

11

down on Adam like no one's business. Still, it got him out and about, didn't it, and that was something.

Times past, Adam wouldn't have even stepped over the threshold at night. Wankers attacking him when he'd walked home in the dark had him afraid to go out. And he *had* been afraid, more than he'd liked to admit, because, fuck, it wasn't cool to say you were frightened. Not around here anyway.

No, it wouldn't be a wise move. People would use it against him.

This city was rough as arseholes. Just two months ago, a bloke had been found murdered in a warehouse, and before that, some nutbag had fed drugs to innocent people in order to make them go out and kill. The world was a messed-up place, no doubt about it, and Adam wanted out of the rat race more than anything.

He shivered, a raindrop sneaking inside his collar and dripping down his neck. Damn weather ought to sod the hell off. Six days it had been raining, with no indication it was going to let up. They reckoned there'd be floods before long, insurance companies shitting bricks at the anticipated payouts. Good job Adam lived in a high-rise then, wasn't it, and as for home insurance... It wasn't like he could afford it.

One day he'd get a job instead of relying on Dane to pay the rent. All right, Dane had moved in when Adam had lost his job because of...well, because of what had happened, but it couldn't go on indefinitely. Adam felt guilty every time Dane dipped into his pocket, money for this or money for that, always something that needed paying for, but Dane insisted he didn't mind.

Adam glanced at the sky. Oddly, it wasn't that dark, despite it being past midnight. The clouds hung low—looked as though they were sitting on the rooftops—all fat grey bellies and puffy arses. The moon shone from between two dirty great cotton balls, its pewter-coloured face somewhat angry compared to the usual smiling effort.

Adam huffed out a short laugh, shaking his head. Like the moon was a real man. Jesus.

The door to the mini-mart clacked open, giving Adam a bit of a start. Loud or sudden noises did that to him, and as he turned to see if Dane was on his way out, he wondered if he'd ever get over this shit. Kevin, Dane's workmate, lifted one hand in greeting then yanked his hood over his head, scarpering down the road. Waste of time, that. He'd be soaked by the time he got home.

Adam stared at the shop. The lights still blazed inside, yet it had closed over half an hour ago. He gave the door a push, expecting it to be locked, but it opened with the same clack it'd made when Kevin had left. The heater above the door blasted a welcome hot breeze, and Adam shivered again, rainwater falling from his hair and into his eyes.

He gazed around, hoping to catch sight of Dane, but he was either in the office securing the takings or in the storeroom. Either way, it was a bit mental leaving the door unlocked like that, considering the dodgy element who lived around there.

"Dane?"

He waited a few beats for a response and, after not getting one, faced the door, lifting his arm to snap the bolts across. They slid into place easily, and he peered through the glass, moving his hand to grab the string that pulled the blinds down.

It took a second or two for it to register that someone in a black balaclava stood on the other side, sawn-off held in gloved hands, fleshy lips slack in the sideways-oval mouth hole.

Adam's legs went. His bollocks drew up, and a scream brewed in his chest, but his lungs strangled the fuck out of it. He willed the scream to come out, or at least some form of noise so Dane knew what was going on, but nothing. He backed away, gaze fixed on that shotgun, as though if he didn't look away from it the thing wouldn't be used. The burly bastard holding it tucked it under his armpit and took aim.

Adam darted to the right, hiding beside the floor-to-ceiling shelf unit in front of the window that held breakfast cereals and chocolate digestive biscuits. He'd bought a packet of those the other day, had fancied them with a hot cup of tea and a good read of the newspaper.

Funny how crap like that came to mind when you were scared shitless.

He backed down the aisle, thinking that if he got to the other end he'd be able to run like hell to the rear of the shop, warn Dane, and call the police. Memories from before came, and he batted them away—if he let them run free he'd be as good as dead. That bloke out there could still see him from where he was, could still shoot through the glass and kill Adam's sorry arse.

Adam legged it, scooting around the corner, almost going arse over tit from his shoes being so wet. He ran to the back of the shop, nudging an end unit holding cheese Doritos and jars of salsa dip. They went flying, glass smashing behind him, and all Adam could think about was getting to Dane, getting to where he was safe.

He plunged through the storeroom door, spotting his brother hunched over a large cardboard box, clipboard in hand, pencil clamped between his teeth. Dane looked up and removed the pencil, slipping it behind his ear. He stood, mouth open ready to speak, and must have registered the fear on Adam's face. He snapped his mouth closed.

"There's a man. A fucking man!" Adam's chest burned.

"Aww, come on now." Dane stepped forward, dropping the clipboard into the open box. "You can't keep doing this every time you see a bloke in the dark. I told you before, it was a random attack, it—"

"There's a man! Shotgun. Balaclava." Adam jabbed his thumb in the air over his shoulder, glancing that way to make sure the bloke wasn't behind him.

"Fuck." Dane's face paled, and he strode past Adam, yanking the door open and going down the corridor to the office.

Adam followed, trailing him right up the arse. Dane stared at two monitors on the desk, one showing the back entrance, the other showing the front, then turned to Adam.

"There's no one there," he said.

"Call the police anyway." Adam leant on the desk, peering at the screens. "He was right there!" He stabbed a finger at the image of the shop door.

"All right, calm down."

Dane picked up the phone and dialled. Adam clenched his teeth in an effort to stave off the shivers rampaging all over him, folding his arms across his middle to give himself a bit of comfort. It had worked in the past, when he was alone at home and thought he'd heard something— someone—outside their front door. It had helped calm him, get things in perspective.

It didn't help now.

His bladder distended, and if he didn't watch it he'd let out a stream of urine. He'd done that in the past, too, pissed all over himself, ashamed at the way his body reacted to even the slightest 'off' noise. He should have gone to see a therapist like Dane had said, but that meant admitting he was mental, that he had a problem, and Adam wasn't, didn't.

He ducked under the table, overreacting now the gunman had gone, but he couldn't help it. Snuggled in the corner, he took deep breaths and listened to Dane talking to the police. The call seemed to take an age.

A loud hammering came from the front of the shop, and Adam jumped, banging his head on the underside of the desk. His heart stuttered, stopped for a few seconds, then restarted with a God-awful beat that was too fast and hurt too bloody much. He gulped, lungs constricting and not allowing any air in, and panicked, flailing his arms and whacking his heels on the floor.

"It's the police already," Dane said, hunkering down and peering at him. "It's okay, it's the police."

Adam's lungs inflated and, nauseated, he fisted his burning eyes. Adrenaline surged through him, sending him lightheaded, disoriented. He blinked, seeing Dane as a blurry shape.

"They stayed on the phone the whole time," Dane said. "And now I have to let them in, all right? You coming out?"

Adam shook his head. He drew his knees up, curling his arms around them, and waited for the pulse in his throat to stop its incessant, deafening throb.

"Okay." Dane stood and walked to the door. "I'll be back in a second."

Adam wanted to call out, to tell him to be careful, but his tongue was stuck to the roof of his mouth. He rested his head back, staring at the underside of the desk at a hardened nub of chewing gum someone had stuck there. It reminded him of school, of being a kid again.

Who said when you grew up you didn't get scared anymore? Who said things got better?

In no time, the office door swung open. Dane's feet were accompanied by four more—encased in shiny black shoes with droplets of rain on them.

"Does that work?" a man said.

"Yeah. You want me to rewind it?" Dane asked.

"Please. And where's the person who saw the gunman?"

"Um, he's under there."

Adam felt all kinds of a prick, but he was fucked if he could make himself come out. One pair of the black shoes moved, came to a stop in front of the desk, and creaked.

A police officer hunched down and looked at him. "You all right there, son?"

Adam nodded.

"Gave you a bit of a scare, did he?"

"Yeah, just a bit. Like before." He hadn't meant to say that last bit.

"Like before?"

"Yeah. I was attacked..." *Why tell him that?*

"Ah, I see. Right. You okay to come out, tell us what happened?"

"About what happened before, or...?"

"No, just now."

Relief bled into Adam's system—he didn't fancy reliving that other time again—and he found the courage to crawl out. He stood, embarrassed, and perched his arse on the corner of the desk. Knitted his fingers. Twiddled his thumbs.

"There he is," the other officer said.

Adam glanced across to the door sharply. A female officer stood there. She stared at a monitor, walking towards the desk, and pursed her lips.

"It's the same man as the others," she said.

"Right, son." The male officer pulled out a notepad. "If you could just tell me what he did, although I could probably tell you."

Adam frowned.

"We've had a lot of incidents like this. He does the same thing every time, but I need to hear it from you just the same."

Adam didn't want to tell them, didn't want the images to come back into his head, but he pushed himself, words pouring as fast as the rain had.

After waiting for Dane to clear up the Doritos and dip and lock up, the police then gave them a lift home.

Once inside their flat, Adam thought he'd feel safe, but he didn't. It wasn't as though by being in your own home the memories went away, was it? They were with you, in your head, and no amount of hiding was going to cut it.

He went into the kitchen, exhaling a steady breath at hearing Dane locking up, and flicked on the kettle. He picked out two mugs and busied himself with the mundane task of making instant coffee so he didn't have to think too hard.

Thinking hard hurt more than your head sometimes.

"You okay?" Dane asked.

Adam stared.

The kettle clicked off, bubbles raging about inside it, steam huffing from the spout. It brought Adam back to reality.

"I can't fucking live here anymore," he said, and the sudden conviction that he couldn't, he really couldn't live here, smacked him full force. "This flat, this fucking *place*..."

"I know. I know. I'll look into it. A fresh start somewhere else, yeah?"

Adam nodded. "Somewhere quiet, without all this bullshit. Too many people here, too much danger. Just...too much everything."

"All right. It'll be all right. I'll take care of it."

CHAPTER THREE

Dane and Adam were going to view a potential property. Dane had chosen a small hamlet called Lower Repton outside the city, close enough that they could visit when needing to do a big food shop but far enough away that a million miles might as well separate the two places. It was nothing more than a single road, cottages in a row on each side and a Cotswold stone pub called Pickett's Inn sitting on the corner, having seen better days by the looks of it. Adam reckoned it might fall down if a storm had the idea of howling through the street.

Why Dane had chosen Lower Repton, when it was still the subject of so much speculation with regards to those Sugar Strand drug murders, Adam didn't know. Maybe because this place was in the middle of nowhere Dane thought they'd be safer, regardless of what had happened here.

Adam relaxed as soon as he saw the small cottage they were thinking of renting, number two, with its whitewashed outer walls, higgledy-piggledy slate roof, and a sign beside the front door that read Reynolds' Gaff. Apparently a murder had occurred here, in the main bedroom, but any clue there had been a killing had been removed, the room bright and airy, belying the fact something grotesque had taken place.

Despite that, all the tension that filled him from the city attack and the recent happenings at the mini-mart drifted away, leaving him free of worry for the first time in quite a while. Sadly, it returned when they went back to their flat. Like a dose of the clap, it itched.

Lower Repton felt different, the people they'd encountered more laid-back, not one of them giving funny looks after they announced they were moving there. Well, no one except an old lady who lived over the road, a bit of a nosy mare if ever there was one, but she didn't seem like she'd do them any harm. Even though the tiny place had been rocked recently, everyone appeared to be getting on with things, getting back to normal. Maybe city dwellers had a pack mentality, the majority following the loudest voices instead of the quiet ones inside them. He didn't know, but he was glad to be getting the fuck away from it, them and the knot of fear that prevented him from moving on with his life.

The city was far behind them. They'd been in the cottage just over a week, Dane and Adam working for a local farmer, helping out with whatever jobs needed doing. Dane had said he'd sort things out, and he'd come through faster than Adam could have imagined. It felt like they'd lived in Lower Repton for longer than they had. What had gone on in the city was a distant memory, something that had almost wrecked another man in another time but the attack had been too brutal, the words spoken too harsh for him to erase them fully.

He'd heard through the grapevine that someone had assumed, because he lived with a bloke, that he was gay.

Finally, the last of the packing boxes empty, Adam flattened them into large squares ready for the recycle collection. He supposed their old mates in the city would take the piss out of the way Adam and Dane had settled into village life, but really, did he give a shit?

No. Where had those mates been after he'd been accosted in that alley? None of them had cared beyond hearing about it for the first time. They hadn't wanted to deal with the aftermath, and when Adam and Dane hadn't gone out clubbing with them like they used to, when they weren't fun any longer, those friends had taken a huge step back. Still, what they thought wasn't his concern now. Quality of life and peace of mind mattered far more than anyone's opinion.

Outside in the back garden, he wedged the cardboard behind a large green wheelie bin and looked around at the shadows. They didn't freak him out like before, where people could jump out at him or lurk about doing things they shouldn't bloody well be doing. Drug pushing, fucking against walls, meeting to work out the best way to do people some damage. The whole ethos of a place like that had always bothered him, but, as usual, he'd never thought anything bad would happen to him.

He'd been so wrong.

Who knew walking home after a few beers could leave him broken and bleeding on the ground, a spiteful wind whipping around him as though Mother Nature was also in on the act? Everything about that night had been wrong anyway, from the sour-tasting beer he'd sworn was off, to the general atmosphere in The King's Arms being fraught with tension. People were antsy, pissed off at the end of a long week when they should have been ecstatic the weekend was there. He remembered thinking that was odd, how everyone had frowns and spoke in sharp, clipped tones.

He wished he'd listened to what his intuition had been trying to tell him instead of brushing it off as insane thoughts. That he'd got mad ideas because he'd been tired and his mind had decided to mess him about. He had too many what-ifs, that was the problem. Dane had told him recently that the past couldn't be changed, so there was no use mulling over it, not unless it helped him to mend himself and move on.

Maybe he'd given someone a weird look that night. Maybe he'd stared a little too long at the wrong person on the wrong day. They'd convinced themselves he was gay, so to them, they were justified in what they'd done. Whatever, that gang of blokes had taken exception and followed him out of the King's. At first, Adam hadn't taken any notice, thinking the men were on a bender, heading to the next pub along the high street, but when he'd reached the end and they were still behind him, he'd got a bit worried. His heart rate had accelerated, his legs had gone weak, but he'd called himself a silly bastard and carried on walking. Like a group of blokes would want to follow him anyway.

He'd told himself they were on their way home, just happened to be going the same way as him, and he'd carried on, head down, hands jammed in his jacket pockets. In Kitchener Street, two roads away from the flat, the men had shortened the gap between them. They'd talked about duffing someone up and making them regret they'd ever lived, and he'd felt sorry for whoever they'd had in mind for punishment. It couldn't have been him, though, because he didn't know them, hadn't done anything to upset them. Regardless, he'd stupidly darted down an alley between houses that led to his street, his safe haven, thinking he'd get back quicker that way.

The men had been on him before he'd even made it halfway down, kicked the shit out of him, and had strode off as though they'd done nothing wrong. That part had struck him as the worst, even more so than the beating. How could some people do that and not feel guilty? Pissed up on alcohol or not, it wasn't normal to act like that. Adam had rolled onto his side and watched them leave the alley the same end they'd entered, laughing and jostling, the streetlights giving them an orange aura. They'd looked weird. Alien.

He'd stayed put, bones and muscles hurting, his mouth so puffy and full of blood he couldn't scream. His whole body had ached, and he'd had a bit of trouble fully processing things. It had all happened so fast. One minute he'd been walking home, the next he was on the wet ground in an alley that stank of cat and dog piss, knowing he couldn't get up because his leg didn't feel right, like it didn't belong to him. Numb. Bent.

An old granny had stumbled upon him the next morning, shaking him awake, bending over him with an expression of pity mixed with horror.

Again, things had occurred in quick-time—the ambulance had come, he'd been loaded into it—and he'd found himself at the hospital, cleaned up and in a gown with a fuck-off great slit up the back. How the hell had he managed to get himself in this mess? Unable to piece things together in any form, he'd drifted back to sleep, uncaring whether he woke again.

When he'd next opened his eyes, Dane had been sitting beside the bed. *Then* Adam had wanted to stay awake, to never sleep again, to always be on alert for arseholes who'd had a mind to do someone in, just because. And he hadn't slept properly ever since—well, until they'd moved to Lower Repton.

Today had been a long one, their Saturday taken up with the last of the settling in. He stared at the same sky he'd always stared at his whole life, yet it appeared different. The stars were brighter, and less cloud coverage scudded across the bright, silver-quarter moon. Dane was inside, putting up a shelf over the head of their beds so they had some place to put their things. Phone. A book.

The sound of a hammer then the use of a drill drifted to him.

He looked out past the water-logged grass and hedges at the bottom of the garden and squinted at a series of bobbing lights in the distance. Car headlamps? They drifted from left to right as though a string of traffic travelled, a set of several cars all going to the same location.

If Adam knew the area better he'd be able to judge where the cars might be going, but the road to the city was the only one he knew and went in the other direction from the front of the cottage. The lights winked out in twin sets one after the other, and, curiosity getting the better of him, he went upstairs to the back bedroom so he could get a better look.

From this height, he made out the shape of a barn, the flicker of strong-beamed torches briefly lighting patches of it—red bricks, a doorframe, a grey-tiled roof? He wasn't entirely sure from this far out, but his imagination liked to fill in the blanks. Every so often the head and shoulders of figures broke the backdrop of dark grey, the people partially obscured behind what appeared to be hedges. The moonlight gave them an eerie appearance. What the hell were they doing out there? He was pissed off with himself for not having studied the landscape more in the daylight. That should have been the first thing he'd done, what with his need to make sure he'd be safer living out here. He'd been so taken by the feel of the place, though, at how he felt so much calmer, that gazing at their surroundings hadn't entered his head.

Dane stopped hammering and using the drill, and a few beats of silence ensued, then he padded up behind Adam.

"What are you doing in here?" he asked.

"Look." Adam nodded at the window. "What d'you think they're doing?"

"Fuck knows. Can't say I give much of a shit." He paused for a second or two, then said, "That shelf was a right bastard to put up."

"It looks weird."

"What, the shelf? Didn't think you'd even been in to have a gander yet."

"No. Them. Those torches, see?" A skewer of fear twisted in Adam's gut. "A few minutes ago they pulled up in cars. From what I could see, about six of them. Cars, I mean. Now they look like they're trying to find something. I wonder if they're one of those groups who go out with metal detectors. They might need to do it in the dark cos the land belongs to someone and whatever they find wouldn't really be theirs."

"Does it matter?" Dane stroked his chin.

"Well, yeah. Not the metal detector thing, though. But what if they're up to something? I thought we were safe here—"

"We are. You sure you're not creating a worry that doesn't exist? I'm not being funny, but you've been fretting for so long, that now you don't need to..."

"You think?"

"Maybe," Dane said.

Whether he was or wasn't, this still didn't sit right with Adam. He needed to make sure they were okay. The fear of the past would always be with him, and since they'd been here and he'd felt so much better, he didn't want his new idyll ruined.

"How far out d'you reckon they are?" he asked.

29

Dane pressed his hands to the sill and leant forward. His breath misted the glass. He *tsked* and wiped the circle of condensation with his jumper sleeve. It squeaked. "About half a mile, give or take a few yards. Why?"

Adam turned from the torch arcs and looked at Dane. Light spilling in from the hallway lit the right side of his face, while moonlight lit the left. Dane frowned, and his mouth was downturned, concern etched not only in his features but in his rigid pose.

"Should we go out there?" Adam asked.

Dane sighed and dropped one hand from the sill, letting it dangle beside him. "Are you serious or fucking me about? It's dark, it's getting late, and we're new around here. We don't really know where we're going or what goes on. Maybe there's some kind of barn dance or whatever the hell village people do on a Saturday night. I don't know, maybe they're searching for a lost dog."

Dane always spoke sense, but niggles of doubt still gnawed at Adam's nerve ends. Something was off, and it wasn't his overactive imagination either. He liked to think that since the attack his senses had sharpened, his instincts making up for buggering off that night and leaving him to become a victim. Except they hadn't, they'd warned him in good time, he'd just chosen to ignore them.

"But we know the general direction," he said. "I just want to see what they're doing. To know it isn't anything iffy. I won't sleep otherwise, and if it's something dodgy, we'll leave them to it and—"

"It won't be anything dodgy." Dane stared out of the window again.

"But how do you know? You said yourself we're new around here."

The huge sigh that gusted out of Dane let Adam know in no uncertain terms he was pissing his brother off. Adam knew he could be a pain, but although Dane tried, he didn't—couldn't—understand how Adam felt.

"Fuck's sake," Dane said in weary tones, pushing off the sill and walking to the bedroom doorway, dragging his feet. "If it makes you happy, we'll go out there, but I tell you, it's probably nothing we need to know about."

Adam followed him out of the room. "Thanks. And I'm sorry for—"

Dane lifted one hand as he disappeared into his bedroom. "It's okay. I get it."

Adam and Dane sat in the car, engine off, headlights doused. The country lane they were in ran directly to the left of a field. Adam looked across Dane in the driver's seat and out of the window. The barn he'd spotted from their cottage stood in the centre, a black monolith, its size that of any warehouse in the city. The torchlight had gone from outside in the time it had taken them to travel and find the right place, but faded swathes shone through a crack in what Adam assumed was

31

a doorway. Whatever was going on, the people inside didn't feel the need to lock themselves in. Maybe being out in the middle of nowhere they felt safe, that no one would encounter them.

Or maybe they're not doing anything bad.

"We're getting out and having a look, aren't we?" Adam waited for Dane to tense up and try to get out of it.

"Yes, we're getting out and having a look, but if nothing's going on, I really think you need to go and talk to someone."

Adam nodded. "I know. I will."

"You say that, but—"

Adam reached across and pointed at the barn. "What the fuck are they *doing* in there?"

The door had been fully opened, revealing a pale rectangle of light and a stack of hay to the rear. People, two of them, stood in the doorway, their silhouettes somewhat relaxed, an arm each bent at the elbow. They were smoking? Others milled about behind them, naked.

What the hell?

"I don't know," Dane said. "Maybe they're getting the barn ready for some do or other. Whatever, I'm not walking across that bloody field while they're standing there."

"What, getting ready for a do with no clothes on?"

"You don't know that. It only seems that way." Dane scrubbed his chin, the sound of his stubble loud.

"I saw the shape of a limp cock on one bloke."

They waited in tense silence for the couple to go back inside and shut the door. Dane sighed quietly and got out. Adam quickly followed, sliding down a bank into the field. The ground squelched, still suffering from the recent rains, and Adam's boots sank with every step, becoming heavy with caked earth. It was chilly now, more so than when he'd dumped the cardboard in the back garden, and he wished he'd put on a scarf and gloves along with his jacket.

As they neared the barn, its features grew more apparent, and yes, it was made of red brick. About twelve feet from it, Adam got the jitters, the haunting sound of men chanting lifting the hairs on the back of his neck. Their voices were low, without any form of melody, a boring drone that was sinister as fuck. His instinct kicked in, telling him they ought to get hell away from there, yet even though he was scared, he wanted to stay.

"Wait," Adam whispered, reaching out to grip Dane's wrist. "I'm... I just need a minute."

Dane stopped walking, and Adam stood beside him, heart beating an uneven rhythm that reminded him of when he'd watched those men leave him injured in the alley. He stared at the barn, the light filtering through the door crack brighter now, and took a deep breath.

Think. Why would men be naked in there?

He had no idea, but if it was nothing more than some orgy, then at least the voice of his instinct urging him to investigate would shut up.

CHAPTER FOUR

Adam took hold of the barn door and pulled it open a little more. It was skew-whiff on its hinges, like it had hung there for years and had grown warped from the weather. He grimaced, waiting for a creak or whine to give them away, but none came. Dane crouched and shifted in front of Adam so they could both see into the barn.

No one was in there.

What the fuck?

Torches had been propped strategically, as if whoever had placed them there wanted to spotlight the centre. Shadows hulked around the edges, thankfully keeping Adam and Dane in darkness, too. Adam got the uneasy feeling he was in the wrong place at the wrong time—again.

"Where did they go?" he whispered, resting his fingertips on Dane's shoulders, disturbed his legs were shaking.

Dane shrugged. "No idea, but I don't see the point in us being here. Nothing's going on." He moved to rise then lowered again.

Something shifted in the far corner, a darker blob of shadow, and Adam took a step back, hoping the security of the darkness outside would further shield him. The torchlight didn't reach the doorway, but that was beside the point. Being spotted wasn't something he wanted to happen. People were unpredictable. For all he knew, those naked fuckers could turn nasty, come out, bare or not, and give him and Dane a good beating. Out here in the middle of nowhere, they wouldn't be seen, and when those people had left, Adam and Dane might be left unconscious, not found for hours.

A bald man walked into the light at the centre. He closed his eyes, face raised to the rafters, and lifted his arms. He hummed, and more bald men joined him, creating a circle, their hands linking them together. They reminded him of those cut-

36

out paper dolls he'd made at school, except these ones had dangling dicks and bollocks.

Adam quietly knelt behind Dane. "This is so weird," he whispered.

Dane turned his head to speak over his shoulder. "Who would have thought crap like this went on, eh? Maybe it's some country ritual or other."

Dane snorted, and Adam's gut clenched. Had they been too loud?

They didn't appear to have heard him, each man emitting the same hum as the first. It sounded like bees, a whole swarm of them, the noise thick and buzzing, going through Adam's skin until goosebumps sprouted all over him. A sensation squirmed in his ears, as though the very bees he'd thought of were crawling around inside, and he swallowed to make it go away.

The men swayed. Muscles in their legs undulated beneath their skin. The humming grew louder, and Adam was sure he heard a pained whimper, muffled by the strange buzz. He cocked his head at Dane, checking if it was him. He didn't appear upset at all, just shocked.

"Did you hear that?" Adam whispered.

"What?" Dane asked.

"That whimper."

"No."

It came again, louder this time.

"There. You heard it then, yeah?"

"Nope."

"Help me!"

"Who the fuck said that?" Tension spread into Adam's body, and he blinked as though it would help establish the owner of that voice.

"Who said what?" Dane frowned, gaze still riveted ahead.

"'Help me'. Someone just said it."

"I didn't hear it." Dan lifted a finger. "Would you look at the size of that man's dick? The one right opposite. Jesus!"

"They're going to hurt me..."

"Oh fuck. Please tell me you heard that, Dane."

"I just told you I didn't."

"Not that! Someone said something else. That the men are going to hurt them."

Dane pursed his lips and looked directly at Adam. "Oh, behave yourself." He laughed quietly.

"I heard it. Maybe you would have as well if you weren't so busy gawping."

Dane wasn't usually such an arsehole. Adam remained silent, knowing damn well he'd heard that voice—a man—as if he'd spoken right beside him.

Just to make sure he hadn't, Adam glanced about. Nothing but darkness beyond the barn door. He stood, the urge to investigate strong.

Dane stared up at him. "What are you doing?"

"I'm going to see if anyone else is out here."

"Not on your own, you aren't."

Adam walked towards the right-hand, outside corner of the barn. That voice had come from a frightened person, and courage had settled inside Adam, pushing his own worry aside. It felt strange not to cower away from confrontation or the unknown, but he acknowledged that he might be getting better now, that Lower Repton had been a good choice.

Apart from what was going on tonight.

He picked up sounds of Dane following—maybe that helped with the courage a bit—and rounded the corner. More of the same field greeted him, although what he'd expected, he didn't know. Well, he did, if he were honest. He thought he'd find whoever that voice belonged to. Some bloke huddled against the barn, waiting for Adam and Dane to rescue him.

The attack on Adam had got to him in so many ways. Maybe no one was out here after all. Maybe he'd imagined they were about to hurt someone because, shit, that was what a band of men meant to him now.

Fear. Hurt. Pain.

Adam shook the thoughts away and continued walking, heading for the rear of the barn. He peeked around the corner. Cars, dark shapes, only their windows and roofs discernible, were parked in a row. So he had been right earlier. He dug his mobile out of his jeans pocket and moved forward. Selecting the torch application, he moved between each car and inspected their insides.

No one. Nothing but the usual paraphernalia— maps, empty juice bottles, the odd crumpled crisp or sweet packet. A newspaper.

"There's no one out here," Dane said.

"Well, I heard someone, and nobody can tell me different." Adam stared at the back of the barn.

A smaller, red-brick building had been tacked on as though an afterthought. Its dark slate roof reached halfway up and sloped so the overhang rested a couple of feet above a single wooden door, pale, possibly from being bleached by the sun.

"Help me!"

A shiver wended up Adam's spine, and his knees weakened. He broke out in a cold sweat. The voice had been *right there.*

Inside his head?

"You heard it that time, didn't you? Tell me you did, or it means I'm going mental."

"Um, no, I didn't, and if you don't pack it in, I'm going back to the cottage." Dane shook his head and made to walk away.

Adam reached out and stopped him. "Just bear with me. There's someone in that sodding building." He pointed to the add-on. "Got to be. Otherwise, why did I hear some bloke speaking again?"

Dan lifted his hands then lowered them to slap against his thighs. "Yes, I'm sure there *is* someone in there. There's also quite a few someones in the other bloody building as well. Maybe that's where they came from, where they got undressed. Who the hell cares? Let's just go back and see what they get up to."

"Hurry. There isn't much time."

40

Adam ran to the door, his heart thudding. A padlock hung off a rusty chain, the door open a smidgen. He pulled it back, seeing only the same murky gloom as outside. Everything looked a deep shade of grey, from the walls to the dirty floor. One hay bale, the huge cylindrical kind, sat on its circular arse in the corner. How the hell had something that size fitted through the door? Then he spied a set of double doors—undoubtedly leading into the barn proper—which answered his question.

He flashed his phone torch beam around the interior. Other than the hay bale and a wooden pole going from floor to ceiling in the centre, nothing else occupied the space.

"Quick," Adam said.

He legged it, stuffing his phone away and skirting the corners of the building in double time. Out of breath at the front doors, he leant one hand on the brick beside them and bent his head to get his breathing back to normal.

"Christ," Dane whispered beside him.

Adam looked into the barn, his face hot and limited oxygen going inside him. He managed to sniff in a huge helping of air, relieved as fuck his lungs filled and the tension in his throat eased. He swallowed then blew out.

The men still hummed, still stood in a circle, but they no longer held hands. Another sat on his haunches in the centre, blindfolded with a strip of black fabric tied at the back in a knot. Adam had a clear view as the man was side-on. What appeared to be a sock had been stuffed in his mouth. His wrists were bound behind his back with mean-looking thin rope, the kind that chafed every time you moved. This man wasn't one of the originals—he had hair—and something inside Adam said this bloke had been in the lean-to, that this was the one who'd been calling out for help.

How the fuck did I hear him from here when he was out the back, though?

Adam frowned, unable to come up with an answer—one that at least made sense.

He bunched his eyes closed for a few seconds to stave off the thought that he had some kind of bloody psychic shit going on here. A knock or two on the head didn't bring on that kind of ability, did it?

He concentrated on what was happening in front of him. Were the standing men in a trance? They did have glazed eyes, and that humming was going right through him.

"I know you're out there. Please, stop them. I don't want to be here."

Adam started, the voice so loud this time he glanced at each man in turn to see if they'd heard it, too. It appeared they hadn't—they continued to hum and sway. He gave Dane a sidelong peek, and it seemed he hadn't picked up on the plea either.

"What the hell is going on here?" Adam muttered.

"Looks like some gay fun to me." Dane widened his eyes.

They lapsed into silence, staring ahead.

CHAPTER FIVE

The main bald man stepped forward, raising his arms as though in supplication. He was hairless all over, which gave him an alien vibe. Adam frowned and studied him, squinting to see if the man had any eyebrows. He did, thick black slashes that appeared out of place on the otherwise sleek and shiny body. He put his hands

43

on the bound bloke's head, massaging with his fingertips. Humming from the outer circle grew louder.

The fella with hair didn't appear to be afraid.

Abruptly, the humming stopped, yet the sound rang on in Adam's ears as residual fuzz, albeit quieter. The silent men remained in place. Their ages ranged from early twenties to forties. They were an odd bunch, people he wouldn't have put together if he'd been told to select folks who gathered for a sexual whatever the fuck this was.

The main bald one raised a hand to the side, and another stepped from his position and into the circle, handing him a whip. He moved to stand behind the kneeling man and cracked a hurtful blow across his spine.

"I think we ought to go," Adam whispered.

"Please, help. Don't leave me. If I call out, if I ask them to stop, they said they'll go after my family..."

"What the fuck?" Adam muttered.

Totally Hairless had stepped back to allow another man a chance at whipping. He only struck once then handed the crop to the next man. It all happened so fast, and by the time Adam could process it properly, the whip had been given to everyone and was now back with the main man. Red welts, raised and angry-looking, marred the kneeler's back. He was fully hunched over now, forehead touching the floor, but his torso bobbed, as though he was silently crying.

"Oh God. Oh God, it fucking hurts..."

The circle of men converged, hauling him to his feet. They appeared as a swarm of nakedness, a mass of pink flesh.

Adam took a deep breath. "He said if he didn't let them do what they wanted they'd hurt his family."

Dane almost laughed too loudly. "Really?"

"We need to get out of here," Adam whispered.

He turned and walked across the field towards the road, Dane beside him. Adam's thoughts went to that voice and what had been said. He shrugged, unable to come up with a reasonable explanation for it. He'd put it down to his overactive imagination, a leftover from his attack, where he fancied the group of men as sinister when all they were doing was indulging in a fantasy.

He couldn't very well put it down to anything else, could he?

Back at the cottage, he climbed into bed, the dregs of what he'd seen lingering in his mind. He turned onto his side, still getting used to sleeping in a strange room. He wondered how long it would take before this place would truly feel like home.

He drifted and waited for that final curtain of sleep.

Just as it fell, he thought that voice spoke again, but the sandman was stronger than Adam's urge to fully digest what he'd said.

"You left me. It's over. All over now..."

CHAPTER SIX

Oliver lay in bed and stared at the ceiling, Langham on the other end of the line wanting to discuss the case because he couldn't bloody sleep.

"I wonder what Shields would have made of all this?" Oliver asked, thinking of the now-dead DS who'd treated him them like shit—one of the last coppers to accept that Oliver had no hand in the murders he brought to their attention.

Langham chuckled. "Fuck knows, but if the warehouse murder was something to do with being gay like the victim suggested, Shields would have had a shit fit. Having to solve a gay case would have tipped him over the edge, the homophobic wanker."

Oliver had been on edge since visiting the warehouse corpse, waiting for the next murder to occur, wondering, every time the phone rang, whether that call would be the one to send them out to another location. The deceased—Thomas Brentworth, they'd discovered—was an openly gay man. Since he'd spoken to Oliver in the warehouse, it was like he'd vanished into the place spirits went when they were happy to be dead, nothing to remain around for, no urgency to see his killer—or killers—brought to justice.

There were no clues that anyone who shouldn't have been there had occupied the warehouse—no hairs, no fibres, nothing. The only fingerprints found were those of the men who worked there during the day, each one with an airtight alibi.

"How long do you think it'll be before the next one happens?" Oliver asked.

"I was just about to ask you the same question. And before you say it, I know you can't find out. It was going to be a pondering query, not a direct order for you to tell me the answer, to know the answer."

"It's different now, though. The feelings I get, I mean. It's like... I asked you that question to see what you thought, because ever since we found Thomas, I've felt off."

"Off? You've seemed all right to me."

"Yeah, well, it wasn't something I could pinpoint at first. Was just mulling shit over, thinking about whether Thomas was going to make himself known again, and it struck me just now that it wouldn't be long and we'd hear more news."

"Struck you like what?"

"I can't explain it. A knowledge. As if I'd been told to watch out for the call, except no one told me, no voice, nothing like that, just a feeling."

"Sounds to me like things are changing with you. Like hearing the voices was only the start of your ability," Langham said. "How do you feel about that? Make you uneasy?"

"Nah, it's all right. What's a few new senses added to the mix, eh? I may as well have the whole psychic deal, it can only help."

"True. Anyway, goodnight."

"Night." He dropped his phone on the nightstand.

The water boiler in the airing cupboard beside his bedroom gurgled like a kettle, telling him it was just after midnight, the Economy 7 kicking into life. There'd be enough hot water soon for him to take a shower if sleep wasn't forthcoming, or maybe he'd have a long soak in the bath. Something wasn't right if he couldn't sleep, and it didn't take much working out to know what. A nagging *thing* in his head pestered, depositing information without a voice, without pictures, just dumping it so Oliver knew about it as if it had always been there.

Someone had been killed tonight, in a warehouse.

Except it wasn't a warehouse. It looked like one, was as big as one—he couldn't see it, but he knew it—and those bald men had been there, preparing a lamb for slaughter.

Why, though? It had to be a ritual of some sort, didn't it? A cult, maybe?

He closed his eyes tighter in order for the info dump to reveal itself some more.

Nakedness. Baldness. Chains? No, not yet, they would come later. The sense came of the victim obeying despite hating every second of...of what?

Oliver strained to see into the darkness behind his eyelids. To get a glimpse of what was going on instead of this appalling blank canvas where the facts were dropped into his head as simply as a penny into a wishing fountain.

Nothing.

"Come on," he whispered. "You can do this."

Nothing.

"Fuck!"

He gritted his teeth, annoyed with himself for not knowing more, wishing whatever had given him the information to give him something else, for him to be able to just seek and find, to know everything so he could stop—

How could he stop what had already happened?

"They left me. It's over. All over now..."

Oliver snapped his eyes open, his body going rigid. He got out of bed, going to the window and drawing back the curtain to look at the street.

"You still there?" he whispered.

"Where?"

"Here, with me."

"No. Yes. I'm with you but still there. I don't like it, don't understand it."

"Where's your body?"

"I'm...I don't know. I can't see."

Oliver swallowed. *Oh God, did they gouge out his eyes or something?*

"No. I couldn't see anything from the time I met that bloke in the club and he put a blindfold on me outside. Said it'd be fun."

"Which club?"

"Samerson's."

Oliver knew it. A gay club in the heart of the city that had live shows every Friday and Saturday night, local bands and whatnot. It had grown in popularity, by all accounts.

"What time was that?" Oliver asked.

"Early evening. Can't remember. I'd been drinking."

"So you can't see where you are now?"

"No. But it smells."

"Of?"

"Rabbit hutches."

"What?"

"Except there's no piss or shit, or that ammonia smell."

"Right."

"What time is it?"

Oliver glanced back at the bedside table to the glowing green numbers of his alarm clock. "Twelve-fifteen."

"Oh fuck. I was meant to be home by eleven. My mum, she'll be worrying."

"Where do you live?" Oliver prayed he'd get the information.

"Twenty-nine Marlborough Avenue."

"And your name?"

Energy drained out of Oliver, and he knew he wouldn't get an answer. He stared back out of the window and down into the street, stupidly thinking that now things had changed for him he might see a manifestation of the deceased beneath the fuzzy glow of the streetlamp, a mournful expression on the face of a blindfolded man who had gone out on the piss knowing he had to be in by eleven—and not making it.

"Jesus fucking Christ..."

Oliver sighed and walked towards the bed. Grabbed his phone. Dialled Langham. "There's been another one."

"Aww, shit. Where is he? It is a he, yes?"

"It's a he, but I don't know where he is. *He* doesn't know where he is."

"So is there a point to me getting dressed yet?"

"Oh yeah, there's a point. He told me where he's been, that he was blindfolded and taken

52

somewhere that smells of rabbit hutches, and I know where he lives."

In the hour before dawn, after going to the station and looking at the CCTV street footage outside Samerson's, knocking on the door of a woman who was about to be told her son might never be coming home didn't sit right with Oliver. They stood on the concrete doorstep of one of seven terraced houses, council-owned or former council housing if their fifties uniformity was anything to go by. Oliver sighed, wondering how the fuck Langham was going to play this one. The deceased—and he *was* dead, they just hadn't found him yet—was Jason Drum, twenty-one years old and fresh out of university where he'd studied to become a social worker. It struck Oliver as doubly sad that a man, so newly a man, too, had wanted to spend his life helping others and now wouldn't be able to.

The city would be a sorrier place without him.

Langham knocked again, blowing a stream of air out through puckered lips, his cheeks ballooning. A light snapped on behind the glass in the door, and a shadowy figure approached, a wide man, Oliver reckoned, over six feet tall. A chain was drawn across, and the door opened to reveal a boxer-like visage that Oliver wouldn't want to join in the ring.

"Yeah?" the man said, hair rumpled, his cheek bearing signs of his pillow, two severe material indents, macabre slashes on his skin.

"Mr Drum?" Langham asked.

"Yeah? Who are you?"

"I'm DI Langham, and this is my associate, Oliver Banks. May we come in?"

Langham produced his ID, and Mr Drum peered down at it, his ruddy face paling. Oliver felt sorry for him. It would pale further before they were finished.

"Um, yeah, yeah. Is this about the call my wife made earlier?" Mr Drum opened the door wider and allowed them access.

"Call?" Langham asked, closing the door as Mr Drum made his way down a slim hallway and waited on the threshold of a room to their right.

"Yeah, Carol phoned in about our son. Meant to have been home by eleven, only he didn't turn up."

Oliver knew what kind of response Carol would have been given.

'Your son is twenty-one, madam, out on the town, probably drunk and has forgotten the time. He'll roll in after the clubs close, no doubt.'

'But he's never done this before. He's always in on time.'

'There's a first time for everything, madam.'

'But this isn't like him. He wouldn't do this!'

'That's what we'd all like to say about our children, but like I said—'

'You don't understand! I know something's wrong.'

54

'Nothing we can do about it until he's been missing twenty-four to forty-eight hours, love, and even then, at his age, it's doubtful something's happened.'

Oliver and Langham followed Mr Drum into a well-kept living room, and Oliver got his first glimpse of who he thought might be Jason. Pictures of a young man in a mortar board adorned the mantel, and photos, younger versions ranging from a baby to a teenager, dotted the mint-green, flock-papered walls. He was loved, then.

"You might want to sit down, Mr Drum," Langham said.

"Oh God... Fuck. Um...yeah. I'll sit down. What...what's happened? Is Jason all right? Had an accident?"

Oliver retreated to just inside the doorway.

Langham sat beside Mr Drum on the pale-blue sofa, perched on the edge ready, Oliver reckoned, to jump up again if the tidal wave of grief sent Mr Drum roaring.

"We have recent information that may indicate your son left the club with an unsavoury character." Langham took a deep breath. "We don't yet know where they went after they were last caught on CCTV getting into a Transit that headed out of the city towards the villages—Strangley, Lower Repton and the like—but we have units out there looking for a van of that description, or sightings of that van."

"Oh God. Carol…she…she knew something was up, and I told her the same as that policeman— nothing to worry about, he'd forgotten the time, he'd be back soon, and I…shit, I was wrong, wasn't I? She said…" A sob caught in his throat. "She said she had a feeling, early evening, it was, that something wasn't right, and I…and I told her it was indigestion from the bloody hazelnuts we'd been eating. She gets that, you know, from hazelnuts. But she said it wasn't the fucking nuts—swore at me just like that, she did—and sat there crying. I didn't know what to do, what was up with her, and I didn't…" He sobbed again. "Didn't even offer her a bloody cuddle."

Oliver swallowed. A thick, hard ball of emotion refused to go down, and he swallowed again, his throat suddenly dry, his heart beating too fast. This wasn't how he'd wanted things to go, watching some poor bastard discover there was a strong possibility something rotten had happened to his kid.

"Was it one of them gay-bashers?" Mr Drum knuckled a tear that brimmed over his lower eyelid.

"We're not sure yet, although there is indication he left with a male." Langham relaxed a little as Mr Drum flopped back. "He was in Samerson's, met the man there."

"D'you think you'll find him?" Hope widened Mr Drum's eyes. "I mean, as far I know, Jason hasn't, you know, done anything yet, just came out to us the other week, as a matter of fact. Wasn't a surprise, because you know your own kid, don't you, and he'd always been different and we didn't hold it against him, we love him just the same, and I'm thinking what a bloody awful thing it would be if he'd found the courage to tell us and went to a gay club for the first time and then this happened and then...and then..."

His tumble of words tore at Oliver's heart, and he turned away from the sight of Mr Drum floundering for something else to say while tears poured down his face and he folded his hands in his lap.

"We're holding out hope that we find him, Mr Drum." Langham stood. "We have a liaison officer on the way, someone who can sit with you, talk to you until we hear more news. Would you like us to wait down here while you tell your wife, or would you prefer us or the liaison to do it?"

"I'll tell her." Mr Drum pushed himself off the sofa and walked towards Oliver. "Yes, I'll tell her. Best coming from me and not no stranger. No offence, like."

He brushed past Oliver and went upstairs.

Oliver waited one second, two, three, then closed his eyes as the wail of a distraught mother ripped through the air.

CHAPTER SEVEN

Instead of stopping where they had the previous night, Dane found the road that led to the rear of the barn.

Dane parked up and glanced across at Adam. "You ready?"

"Yeah, but it feels odd being here in daylight." Adam was wary of them being seen poking around. After all, he'd spotted the headlamps from their cottage, so someone from their street might see them now the sun was up. He hadn't been able to stop thinking about the blindfolded man and had persuaded Dane to bring him here.

Adam opened the car door and got out, thinking that if they looked in the barn and lean-to and no one was about, they could go home. It gave him the creeps, the barn being in the middle of the field like it was, with nothing in it but hay bales. He closed the door and waited for Dane, who didn't bother locking the car up.

"Come on." Adam headed for the lean-to.

"No, the main barn first."

Adam sighed and walked around the front, Dane at his rear. He was surprised at the door being ajar. "You go first." He jerked his head.

"What, you worried they might still be here? The cars have gone ..."

"I know, but... Just...just you go first."

Dane sighed, pulled the door wider, and disappeared inside. Adam took a deep breath then followed. It was quite dark with only the light through the doorway coming in. Adam squinted to get his eyes accustomed to the change. It looked the same but felt different. He supposed it would, being daytime and everything, but a niggling feeling deep inside told him something was wrong. He couldn't explain it, didn't think he should try to when it would only get Dane's back up, but he wanted to go home.

"There's... I don't like it in here." He jammed a hand through his hair and tugged to try to take his mind off the eeriness.

"Fuck me, Adam. It's just a barn."

"Yeah, but it's someone else's property. We shouldn't—"

"You were the one who wanted to bloody come here."

Adam trailed him to the rear door he supposed led to the lean-to. He swallowed, trying to get rid of the idea that they should turn around and walk straight back out. Told himself he was only feeling this way because of what he'd seen here last night. That there was nothing to worry about, no one was going to turn up and find them. No one would ever know they'd been here.

"Oh God. Oh fuck!" Dane slapped his hands on his head and danced from foot to foot.

"What? What is it?" Adam's heart raced, and his mind joined in, thoughts of what was inside the lean-to rushing through his head at top speed. Rats?

"Don't come in here. Just...fuck, don't come in here. Go away. I'll deal with it." Dane made to step back, his hand on the door ready to close it.

Adam ignored him, pushing in to stand beside Dane, the door swinging wide. "Oh Jesus..."

The hay bale was adorned with splashes and streaks of black, like thick slashes of spun sugar. The floor had similar decoration, except there were also arcs, as though the blackness had come from a water hose or the end of an implement. A

61

naked, blood-covered man was chained to the wooden pole in the centre, his features obscured by the same dried darkness. Adam gasped, his breath sticking in his throat, lungs seeming to freeze with his fright. He staggered, one arm out to his side, but there was nothing to brace himself on.

The man's chest... Adam couldn't see any skin colour as the chains holding him up resembled a metal boob-tube. And his legs...they'd been broken. They dangled at odd angles, cracked and jagged shin bones protruding through the skin, snapped sticks in a forest of mulchy blackness. His head had been positioned so it seemed the man's last action had been to glance at the rafters. Adam lowered his gaze. Bile raced up.

The weight went out of him, all but disappeared, and he fell to his knees. Pain raced into his thigh bones, stopping at his pelvis. He retched, trying to come to terms with what he'd seen, the image in his head starker by the second until he didn't think he'd be able to take it anymore. But if he opened his eyes, he'd see the same damn thing. He stood, legs wobbly, his whole body shaking, and placed one hand over his mouth, then took a step forward.

He glanced at Dane, who stared wide-eyed, mouth working but no words emerging. Adam reached out and touched his arm, and Dane wrenched his gaze from the body to look at Adam.

"I *knew* something was wrong. Didn't I *say* that?" Adam said, the words muffled behind his hand. "I had a feeling we shouldn't come back, but at the same time I knew we had to, and when we got here...fuck, I wanted to go home, *needed* to go home..." He glanced at the body again and wished he hadn't. "We have to call the police."

"No." Dane paled. "We'll go home. Forget about this. This is just...this is just way too fucking much for me."

Adam lowered his hand. "What? I don't believe you just said that. A bloke got killed here—look at him, look at the way his throat's been cut!"

"Shit!" Dane rubbed one hand over his mouth, staring at a spot somewhere behind Adam.

"Yeah, shit."

Adam's stomach muscles bunched, and he stumbled through the main barn, the journey seeming to take forever. He made it out into the fresh air, digging in his pocket for his phone, hand trembling way too hard and fast. He rang the police, a rush of words he didn't understand careening out, the dispatcher asking him to calm down, to repeat himself from the beginning, except slower. He tried to do as he'd been asked, but the words tumbled again. He couldn't seem to say what was in his head, in the order it needed to come out. Dane appeared and took the phone, explaining more calmly what they'd found. Adam slumped to the ground, leant his head against the brick of the barn, and closed his eyes.

And remembered the voice as he'd fallen asleep last night.

"Oh God..." Had he really heard that man? Were those the last words he'd ever spoken or thought?

He opened his eyes and focused on Dane who was giving their names and address, pacing up and down. What he said meshed with Adam's thoughts, creating a jumble of sound, overly loud clutter rattling inside his head that he didn't think he could stand for much longer. Fear rose in him. Terror had visited them again, followed them from the city to Lower Repton as though Adam didn't deserve a bit of fucking peace, like he hadn't suffered enough.

Angry—more at himself for his failure to help the man last night than anything—he got up and faced the barn, resting his forearms on the wall. The knobbly surface dug into his skin through his jacket, and he welcomed the distraction. He stared at the ground, kicking at ratty grass, his boot toes striking the brick from time to time.

Dane was still talking, yes-and-no answers, and Adam guessed that, like in the mini-mart, the police were keeping him on the line until they arrived.

Adam pushed off the barn, sucking in air, eager to spot a police car flying along the bottom of the field on the country road. No white car with flashing lights came, but soon another did, unmarked, turning onto the track that led to the barn and speeding along at a clip.

"That was fucking quick," Adam muttered, indicating to Dane that they should go around the back. Then a thought struck him. What if some men from last night were returning? What if that wasn't the police? "Um, we need to get in the car quick. Lock ourselves in."

Dane ended the call and handed Adam's phone back. "No, we don't. That car there apparently has detectives in it."

"He's dead...it's..."

He couldn't finish. He'd wanted to say it was his fault the man was dead, but that would mean bringing up the voice again, and he doubted Dane would be in the mood for that. Round the back, they waited for the car to be parked, Adam's nerves jumping. The detectives got out and strolled over. One introduced himself as Langham, the other his associate, Oliver Banks. Langham was the bigger of the two, and Banks, a slight bloke who had an air of strangeness about him, appeared distant and somewhat agitated. He cocked his head, mumbled something Adam didn't catch, and strode towards the lean-to. He talked to himself and narrowed his eyes as though trying to work something out.

"Don't mind him," Langham said. "Sounds mental, but he's psychic. Talking to dead people makes him come off as weird, but I promise, he's harmless. Now then." He looked at Dane. "Did you call this in?"

"Yes." Dane nodded.

Adam widened his eyes, Langham's and Dane's conversation fading. That Oliver bloke heard voices? Jesus. Was it worth mentioning to him that *he'd* heard a voice, too? He slowly walked over to him. Oliver mumbled and held his hand up. Adam stopped.

"Right," Oliver said. "So these men here have nothing to do with it. Okay. Can you repeat that last bit?" He stared at the sky, frowning. "You asked for help, but they didn't step in, is that it?" He pursed his lips. "I understand. Yes."

Adam fought the instinct to blurt that yes, the bloke *had* asked for help, but he hadn't asked out loud. If he had, though, would Adam have entered the barn and tried to intervene? With all those men there to overpower him? He wasn't sure and felt sick about it, sick over knowing he probably would have just called the police instead and waited in the car until they arrived.

I should have called them anyway. Reported those arseholes for doing what they did.

Hindsight equalled arsehole.

Oliver lowered his hand. "Hello? Are you still there?" He shook his head, peered into the distance behind Adam, then moved to stand in front of him. "Before you say anything, I know."

Adam's heart picked up speed again, the pulse in his throat throbbing fast and furious. "You know what?"

"That you were here last night. That he spoke to you."

"But he didn't—"

"I know *how* he spoke to you, and I know how it feels to tell someone you hear voices and they don't believe you. Me? I hear shit when they're dead. Had the ability as far back as I can

66

remember. Langham there"—he nodded towards the detective and Dane—"won't think you're a nutter or anything like that. Just tell him how it happened, all right? Come on. Over here with me." Oliver tilted his head in Langham's direction. "Tell him what you know."

Adam trailed him back to the detective and Dane. He listened as Dane finished giving his version of events, then told his side of the story. Langham didn't raise an eyebrow, and Adam wondered if it was because he'd given his first reaction to Dane already. Still, something about the man made Adam think he'd heard far worse in his lifetime, and that them watching naked men in a barn was a mild telling compared to others.

"Right," Langham said. "I need to wait here for another detective to arrive, along with the other police officers, and then we can go to your house and discuss this in greater detail. I suggest, if you're asked by officers what happened, you leave out the bit about hearing that voice. We can't explain it, they'll just think you're on your way to the funny farm, and that solves nothing. So, what's your address?"

Dane rattled it off, and Oliver sucked in a sharp breath. Langham looked at him, and something passed between them, an unspoken set of sentences only they heard.

"Well, instead, perhaps we'll find a quiet corner in Pickett's Inn, eh?" Langham said. "I doubt they have much trade going on in there. We shouldn't be disturbed."

"We know about the murder in our cottage," Adam said.

Langham rolled his shoulders. "Do you two mind going inside the barn with us now so you can show us where the body is, or would you rather not?"

"I'd rather not go in there again," Adam said. "Sorry."

"Okay. Go and sit in your car then. Dane?"

"I'll do it." Dane nodded, staring at the ground.

"Good man," Langham said, handing Dane a pair of white booties.

What was the point in Dane wearing them if he'd already been in there?

All three of them now had their feet covered, and Langham led the way towards the front of the barn, Oliver behind them.

Adam stood alone for a while after they'd disappeared around the corner, shivering at the turn his life had taken.

CHAPTER EIGHT

Pickett's Inn was a quiet little place, its outside appearance shouting a big fat lie about how the interior would be. To all intents and purposes, people would be forgiven for thinking the building was on the verge of collapse, with its leaning outer walls and insanely dipping roof. The front door was in need of a fresh coat of wood stain, the old stuff peeling in places, showing a silver-grey beneath. Inside was a different matter. The owners, an elderly couple cheerily introducing themselves as Marge and Brian Dawson, had kept the look of days gone by, opting for barstools studded with fat-topped nails around the seat edges and dainty Elizabethan chairs. They had, they'd said, given in and placed two button-backed burgundy leather sofas against the longest wall, and Adam admired how comfortable they appeared. He didn't hide his relief when Langham made a beeline for them, placing their tray of drinks on the table in front.

Adam and Langham flopped onto the sofa, but Oliver and Dane chose to sit opposite on the chairs. They went through their statements again, Langham writing them out on official police forms this time, checking his notes along the way.

"So, Dane, Adam asked you if you'd heard the voice, yes?" Langham took a sip of his Coke.

"Yes, but I didn't. I thought he was pulling my leg. You know, fucking about because it was dark and he wanted to scare me."

"I won't be writing that bit down about the voice, by the way," Langham said, giving Adam his attention, "but it's interesting. I don't understand how it works for Oliver, how it's even possible to hear the voices of dead people, but he does. It's been proven time and again with the information he receives and the results it produces. But your case, hearing someone who's alive? Christ..."

70

"It's called telepathy," Oliver supplied. "And in Adam's situation, I think there's a touch of empathy, as well as a sense of knowing something was wrong at their return to the barn today, even when the victim was dead. In some cases, empaths—also known as telempaths—can affect the minds of others. Some people are born with their abilities, like me, but others get it later on in life, after a trauma, either to their head or a life-changing, frightening experience. Maybe even a happy experience. I don't know the ins and outs of it, just the basics, but it's interesting stuff. You had anything like that happen, Adam?"

Adam glanced at Dane. "Yes, two things. Trauma to the head and a traumatic experience or two."

"Oh?" Oliver took a deep pull on his drink then put the glass back on a beer mat. "If you don't mind me asking, what happened?"

"No, I don't mind." But he did. Reciting that attack always left him cold. Still, he gave them the brief details and suppressed a shudder, then added the short tale about the mini-mart.

"Fascinating," Langham said, "although I can understand you might not see it that way. Going through what you did was terrible. But, hey, there's a bright side. Hearing that man's voice might just have been a one-off if you're lucky."

Adam laughed, even though he didn't find it funny. It just seemed the right response, something you automatically did in situations like this. Laugh it off, everything's a joke, except it wasn't, was it? He was the one dealing with the fallout from that crap—him and Dane. He hadn't considered being able to hear other people in the future, either, and the thought shit the life out of him.

"There's a way to control it, you know," Oliver said. "Exercises you can do to learn to channel them out. At least that's the case with the dead. Just be thankful you only heard one voice, that you haven't got several at once, all clamouring for your attention. Drives you bloody mad. Sometimes you want nothing more than to just hear your own thoughts." He smiled. "Sorry, that's not the kind of thing you want to be hearing, is it."

Adam smiled, too, suddenly wanting out of there, back to their new life before all this crap had landed on their doorstep. Or at least for Oliver and Langham to leave them in peace. There was only so much Adam could handle, and he was on the verge of breaking down. It had all been too much. To think he'd thought they were safe. Jesus.

"Right." Langham held the clipboard to his chest. "You're free to go home, but be aware that either us or other police officers will want to speak to you again. Remember, keep the voice out of it. I shouldn't be telling you that, but I know from Oliver here it really isn't worth the hassle you'll get. Besides, it isn't relevant." He cleared his throat. "What I must tell you, though, and I'd like you to keep this to yourselves, is we have a strong suspicion this case is linked to another. You heard

72

about the bloke found at the warehouse a couple of months ago?"

Adam nodded. Dane winced.

"Well, it was a similar thing. Similar way of stringing the victim up, the bald men and what have you. Usually, we wouldn't give you information like this, but these two cases may also—and I stress *may*—be linked to the Sugar Strands case."

Adam gulped in a deep breath. Fuck. That had been huge, was still talked about, what with it happening so recently and involving Lower Repton. Drugs making people kill, kids going around murdering people. It was all mental. He didn't understand how anyone could go about killing on purpose. Wanting to.

"Are we in danger?" he asked, stomach coiling into a hard knot—a knot he'd had inside him for such a long time. Yet he'd had a small respite from it, and now that it was back it seemed to hurt more than it had before. All his old fears came rushing back, of being involved in something he didn't want to be in, worrying and looking over his shoulder all the time. Wondering if a knock on the door, even in daylight, would be someone coming to finish him off. If they didn't, the bloody worry would. He wouldn't be surprised if his blood pressure was fucked up.

Langham shook his head. "Your names won't be mentioned in the press, although, with us being here with you today and the discovery only a couple of miles away, I imagine the folks around here will put two and two together. I'll arrange for a police officer to stay outside your cottage until this is over or we find today's discovery isn't linked to Sugar Strands. Because of the way things worked with that case, we know that even though the main players were caught, some drugs may still be out there. Maybe some whacko found a stash of them, realised what they were, and decided to do a bit of experimenting. Or maybe it's nothing like that at all and the latest two cases are linked to each other but not to Sugar Strands. While there's a chance of a disturbed individual out there—or many disturbed individuals—it's best to err on the side of caution."

Langham shrugged. "Better to be safe than sorry, eh? There were no witnesses to the warehouse killing, so the perpetrators perhaps think they've got away with it. But you are our only hope of identifying the men responsible this time." He shook his head again and lowered his clipboard to look at the statements. "About twenty of them, you said. Jesus." He smiled brightly. "Anyway, this is as far as we can go with you for now. Oliver and I have things to do, obviously, and I'm sure"—he eyed the old-fashioned wooden cuckoo clock behind the bar—"you two are hungry and wouldn't mind getting a good night's sleep."

Adam checked the time himself, surprised it was just past five o'clock and it was dark outside the netted windows. Those nets reminded him of his childhood home, when he'd stood at the window and peered through them, the smell of them dusty, that dust going up his nose and bringing on a sneeze. His stomach growled. They hadn't eaten for a few hours, and despite the afternoon's events, he could do with a bite. When they'd discovered the body, he'd thought he'd never want to eat again, but here he was, hungry.

After Langham and Oliver had given out business cards with instructions to call if they remembered anything new, they left.

Adam rose to get a menu and took it back to their table.

"I'm sorry," Dane said.

"What for?" Adam frowned and sat on the chair Oliver had vacated.

"For not believing you. About the voice." He shrugged.

"It's all right. I wouldn't have believed me either." Adam gave what he hoped was a warm smile and held back memories of how he'd thought he was going mental last night. "It gives me the bloody creeps, the thought of it happening again."

"I hope for your sake it doesn't."

As though wanting to erase the events of the day, they lapsed into silence, Adam leaning closer to Dane, opening the menu out so they could browse it together. The pictures of the food were appealing, but he'd bet the real thing didn't look anything like it when it arrived. It never did.

A few more customers came in, and Adam glanced over his shoulder at them, wishing he was them, with nothing more pressing going on other than their recent choice of whether they should stay in or go out to the pub. But he wasn't them, was he, and he'd just have to deal with this shit hour by hour and hope he came out on the other side with his sanity. For all he knew, they had shit of their own to deal with, and coming in here was their way of escaping their troubles for a couple of hours. You just didn't know what trials and tribulations people carried around with them.

Once Dane had made his meal choice, Adam went up to the bar to place their order and get a couple more drinks in. This time he chose pints of lager—the alcohol would help steady his nerves and relax him a little—then returned to find Dane had moved over to the sofa. He looked knackered. Adam sat beside him, putting the pints on the table. The glasses were coated with condensation except for where his fingers and thumbs had been, and dribbles of fluid streaked down to the bases, pooling on the wood.

"Want to talk about it?" Dane asked.

Adam shook his head. His throat was strained from so much chatting.

"Me neither." Dane sighed.

"My throat's dry as a nun's chuff."

Dane chuckled, and they sipped their lagers. Adam's mind was surprisingly blank. He was numb and seemed unable to process anything, so he watched the other customers then took in the sight of horse brasses mounted on the wall in between pictures of what he could only assume was Lower Repton years ago. The same road with the same cottages, only the painting of Pickett's Inn showed a considerably less decrepit building with a proud roof and walls that stood ramrod straight instead of the slouching ones of today.

Their meals arrived, simple fare of steak and kidney pie and chips, and Adam ate without tasting, without thinking of anything at all except jabbing his fork into the food and bringing it to his mouth.

Once full, they stood in unison then left the inn with a nod and a wave to the owners. Outside, the air had turned crisper than it had been when they'd arrived, and Adam hunched his shoulders, raising the collar of his jacket over his ears. It didn't do much to ward off the chill, but it wasn't like they had far to go before they were inside and warm again. They crossed the deserted road, the darkness behind their cottage creepy-looking, a vast expanse that seemingly never ended. Why hadn't he noticed that when they'd come to view the cottage for the first time? He thought of the barn hidden in the distance and blocked it out, determined to get home and make a cup of tea, watch a bit of TV, curtains closed, the world shut out.

They reached home and went inside. Now it felt familiar, like a home should. Welcoming. The warmth was lovely, and he shrugged off his coat, letting the air embrace him. He drew one of the living room curtains across and spotted a car pulling up outside, the headlamps dousing and the interior light going on. Langham had stuck to his promise of a police guard, then.

Adam closed the other curtain then turned. It was best to just forget the copper was out there and try to have a normal evening.

Dane stared blankly. "It'll be all right, you know, bruv."

In bed, the covers drawn up to his chin, Adam sighed and stared at the cream slice of illumination coming in from the hallway. Yeah, he'd been spooked enough to leave the landing light on, not wanting the demons of the night to come and get him. Yet they were here anyway, in his head, flickering like so much badly spliced movie footage, one scene cutting to the next in jagged pieces.

"Fuck!" he whispered and got out of bed.

He padded downstairs to make some tea, sat with it at the kitchen table, and mulled things over. Was the barn killing an isolated case? Was it linked to just the warehouse murder? Were both linked to the Sugar Strands case? Was the latter even possible? The first two didn't pose any threat unless he and Dane identified the men and they had to appear in court or their names were dragged into it. If more men were involved, they could come after them, try to shut them up. But that was a bit far-fetched, wasn't it? It wasn't like they lived in gangster land.

But people from the city do.

78

He clamped his jaw and blotted that thought up as though it was just a spill that could be cleaned away. He did the same with every frightening thought he conjured while examining all the possibilities, and by the time he was done he felt better due to one thing—this time they had the police on their side, actually following things up. This time the case was possibly so big his welfare wasn't classed as something that could be ignored then forgotten. The authorities wouldn't want another victim on their hands, another person's death or disappearance to explain to an already outraged public.

No, he was safe here in this situation.

As though to convince himself of that, he got up and went into the dark living room. He pulled one curtain back a bit and peered outside. The police officer was still there, reading by the looks of it, head bent with a flashlight wedged into one of the spaces in his steering wheel. Idly, Adam wondered if it would be the same copper out there by the time he peeked out again tomorrow, or whether they would silently change over while he slept—if he finally managed to.

CHAPTER NINE

Adam did sleep, thankfully, from around three a.m. until eight. They were due at the farm at ten, their job for the day clearing up pig shit, he imagined, but it was better than hanging around here where he'd let his mind wander to things it was best it didn't wander to. He'd only deal with stuff as it presented itself now, and he was lighter of spirit, his shoulders less heavy.

Dane had left him sitting at the kitchen table, going out to the shop a neighbour had set up in her back room. Lower Repton really was like something out of the past, stuck in its ways and refusing to move on. A shame, then, that the ugliness of the twenty-first century had breezed through, turning everything upside down and giving the residents a massive dose of reality. Shouting in its violent voice that life had moved on, and would you look at that, murder even happened here.

The sound of a key scraping in the lock had Adam turning around. Dane walked into the kitchen, folded newspaper tucked under his arm, a carton of milk in hand. He didn't look happy, a rigid frown firmly in place, his mouth downturned.

"What's up?" Adam asked, refusing to allow the knot of concern in his belly to grow into something more sinister.

"Fucking journalists, that's what, and whoever tells them this shit." He slapped the newspaper on the table and went over to the side to make coffee with jerky, un-Dane-like movements.

"Shit," Adam said.

He wasn't sure he wanted to read the news. Was it sensible to read whatever had been printed? Or was it true that what you didn't know didn't hurt you?

"What's it say?" he asked, thinking it might sound better, gentler coming from Dane. "I mean, is it really bad?"

Dane brought two mugs over and placed them on the table. He slumped into a chair and leant back. The wood creaked. "It doesn't mention us, if that's what you mean." He flexed his jaw. "Not our names anyway."

"What d'you mean? What's the problem?"

"They're calling it the Queer Rites case. It insinuates we're in on it."

"Like how?"

"That two new residents from Lower Repton—I mean, come on, who isn't going to know it's us?—went to the barn to get their jollies then backed out."

"We can deny it—"

"What, deny we're new? Deny the fact a bloody copper's out there in his car? I tell you, I nearly gave the shop woman what for when she pursed her chicken's arsehole lips at me and gave me one of those looks. Bloody old cow."

"What looks?" He didn't need to ask, he knew exactly what looks, but he was stalling, diverting the conversation away from what the news leak could actually mean for them. Moving again. Hiding.

"Oh, you know the kind. I thought we'd found a good place to be at last, but people around here won't be any different to those we left behind, I'll bet. We were stupid to think they weren't the same as every other fucker." He let out a big sigh and rubbed his forehead. "If it was a bigger place we could've got away with it, said it was someone else they were on about, but it isn't, and we can't. This is just one street, for Pete's sake. I'm half expecting us not to have a job when we get there. Villagers don't take kindly to outsiders dicking things up."

Adam hadn't thought of that, but the farmer, Sam Rhodes, was a nice bloke. But supposedly being 'involved' in the barn thing might change his opinion. "We should just take the newspaper up there and show him, tell him what happened. Tell him we're not here to cause trouble…"

"Yeah, I know what you're saying." Dane took a sip of coffee and cringed. "Ugh, I forgot the bloody sugar. But yeah, at least that way we know where we stand instead of waiting for him to find out, get the hump, and sack us."

Adam glanced at the clock on the microwave. "All right, we'll go now."

"We don't start for another hour."

"So? We'll be showing we don't expect to discuss it on work time—providing we still have work there when we've finished telling him."

"Right. Okay. Fuck it, let's get it over and done with."

"All right, lads?" Sam nodded in his usual manner, propping a shovel against an outhouse wall. He wiped his meaty hands down his dirt-stained jeans then crossed his arms over his chest.

"You ready for it today? Looks like it's going to bloody piss down again. It'll make the pig shit all sloppy, but what can you do, eh?" He glanced at the sky and frowned.

Had he heard the news and wasn't bothered, or had he yet to go in for his break and read the paper—if he'd even bought one, that was? Adam couldn't tell. Sam was his normal self.

"Yep, ready for it," Dane said, "but you might not be after what we've got to tell you."

Sam lifted his chin. "You on about that barn murder?"

"Yeah." Dane handed him the newspaper.

Sam took it, sliding it under his arm. "I had the police up here." He pinched one side of his jaw between finger and thumb. "Asked me whether I'd seen a Transit hereabouts. Then they came back this morning. Told me my barn'll be out of use for a bit cos someone had been killed there."

Shit, it was his barn?

"Your barn?" Dane said, eyes wide.

"Yeah. Bit of a bugger that, because I'd only just got it cleared out ready to store stuff in. Course, it isn't the poor bastard's fault he got killed in there, is it, so there's not much I can do but suck it up and wait."

"You read the paper today?" Dane nodded at it and chewed the inside of his cheek.

"Yeah, and what a right load of old crap that is. Reckon this one needs to join mine. In the bloody fire. Look, lads, the only thing that would bother me is if you were in on the killing, and somehow I don't think that's right, do you?"

"No." Adam was relieved he'd finally found his voice.

"'Sides, the coppers told me all about it." He clapped once. "Right, no use us gas-bagging. The chickens need a good clear out, and there's a right big layer of pig shit accumulated over the weekend. You good to be getting on with that?"

"Yes," Adam said.

"On you go then." Sam turned to pick up his shovel. "Oh, and while we're at it, don't you be worrying about those down in your road. I'll soon sort them out. Reckon the only ones who'll give a toss and believe the rags are the old biddy opposite and the one who runs that little shop. Fishwives with nothing better to do, the pair of them. I'm off for a cuppa." He held up the paper. "And this'll go some way to warming my toes in the grate while I'm at it."

Sam traipsed towards his house.

"Well, that was easier than we imagined," Dane said, setting off for the chicken shed.

"You want me to work with you in there, or shall we do the job separately?" Adam called after him.

"On my own," Dane shouted. "Don't fancy company today."

Showered and dressed in clean clothes, Adam lounged on the sofa while Dane finished cooking

86

dinner. Adam's muscles ached—Sam hadn't been joking about the accumulation of shit—and he closed his eyes only to snap them open again when sleep crept up way too fast. He was shattered, a combination of the day's work and the shock from yesterday, he reckoned. He'd ignored the second edition of the newspaper when they'd arrived home and avoided the local news channel on TV. The last thing he wanted was a reminder of what he was trying to forget, but it wasn't that easy, what with the elephant in the room.

He stared at it, a large, two-layered box of Milk Tray on the coffee table, deposited on their doorstep while they'd been at work, wrapped in bright pink paper with a matching bow. Sam had left the farm during their lunch break, saying he had some old biddies to sort out, and had winked when he'd come back, confirming everything was hunky-dory.

"Ought to have been a writer," Sam had said. "Had them eating out of my hand with the tale I told them. As far as they're concerned, you're heroes, got it?"

Adam smiled at the memory and slid the box towards him. Part of him thought he'd choke if he ate any of them, knowing the gift had only been given because someone respected in the community had ensured the rumours were squashed. He had no doubt in his mind that if Sam hadn't visited their street today, quite a few residents would have given them the silent treatment, made things awkward until they eventually moved away.

Still, chocolate was chocolate, but scoffing it wouldn't solve his current problem of Dane giving him the cold shoulder all day. He knew what his brother was thinking: if they hadn't moved here, they wouldn't be involved in this crap.

CHAPTER TEN

Oliver leant his head back against the passenger seat as Langham drove away from Mr and Mrs Drum's for the second time. They'd been to deliver the awful news—well, Langham had delivered it—and left a crumpled couple to try to come to terms with the fact their son was dead and no, they really didn't need to view the body if they didn't want to, but if they did, it might be best to wait a day or two.

Wait for Hank to make Jason pretty again.

"That was...horrible," Oliver said. "I don't ever want to do that again."

"Be thankful you don't have to. I, on the other hand, have it on my list of regular to-dos."

"Every job has its shit points." Oliver massaged the bridge of his nose, hoping the headache that taunted in the back of his skull would fuck off before it had the balls to shift to the front.

"And we've got a shitty point ahead of us now." Langham veered out of the housing estate and headed towards the city's innards.

"Hank?"

"Yeah, Hank, but you can wait outside in the corridor if you'd rather."

Did Oliver rather? He wasn't sure. The morgue hadn't been his favourite place last time, but as with the Sugar Strands case, this one had got to him. It had something to do with him being in the thick of it again, seeing the case unfold, the officers working around the clock to get some kind of lead, and he wasn't sure he should be enjoying, if that was the right word, the change from mere informant to being Langham's 'associate'.

He thought about his editor boss's voice earlier, filled with glee that Oliver wouldn't be coming in to work because he had to assist the police. The barrage of questions—"Do you have anything you can give me yet? You got some information for me before we go to press?"—got Oliver's goat. That was the way of the world, humans had the urge to know every gory detail, but the fact his boss did this for a living and revelled in all the juicy nuggets he could get his hands on wasn't quite right in Oliver's opinion. Would he rather be making endless cups of tea for the journalists or sitting beside Langham now, on their way to see a jolly man who cut open corpses in order to find out how they'd died?

The latter, definitely, although not the going to see Hank part, not seeing Jason Drum laid out on a metal slab, the top of his head cut off as Hank weighed his brain. Oliver wanted to help solve the case, that was all, to give the dead justice so they could move on.

Jason hadn't spoken to him since they'd been to see him at the barn. If it was some kind of ritual killing, then the way Jason had been murdered was an escalation. Thomas hadn't been harmed—discounting strangulation by a thick chain, of course—and there had been no whipping marks on his body, no signs he'd been mistreated prior to his death. But with Adam's and Dane's witness statements and the proof on Jason that he'd been whipped until he'd bled, whoever had done this had upped the ante.

What the fuck would these men do next? And when? How long would they leave it between Jason's murder and the next? Would Adam hear voices from a future victim, and would Oliver be given another info dump—before the person was actually killed this time?

If only that would happen.

Langham pulled up to the morgue's back doors, and the jarring, throaty squeak of the handbrake being lifted pulled Oliver out of his thoughts.

He made a snap decision. He'd go inside the examination room, not wait in the corridor, but *only* in case Jason wanted to speak to him again.

Jason had remained silent, a bloody mess of peeled-back torso, thanks to Hank, and whip slashes. Hank had confirmed the cause of death—another chain strangulation.

Oliver sat in Langham's car now, on their way to a house that would hopefully give them the results Langham hoped for. The Transit had been found, an everyday white bugger with a dented left side and a wonky rear number plate. It sat outside a Mr Littleworth's house, him being the owner, although it had recently been stolen then returned if Mr Littleworth was to be believed. Oliver wondered why the man hadn't reported it as stolen. He asked Langham what he thought.

"He didn't even know at first it had been taken, apparently." Langham cursed as a driver in a green Ford cut him up.

"So what made him realise?"

"The dent in the side. Said—damn these bloody red lights!—it'd been in pristine condition when he got out of it after work Saturday evening." Langham jerked to a halt and stared mutinously at the line of stopped cars ahead. "I swear to fucking

God the fates are against us whenever we start getting leads."

Oliver nodded absently, eyeing the lucky sods opposite who cruised across the T-road in front of them, their traffic lights gloriously green. "So it was taken, used to transport Jason, then returned...when?"

"I can only assume the same night, because Adam said that when they'd been at the barn that night there were only cars parked out the back."

"They must have switched vehicles, used Mr Littleworth's van on purpose. They know what they're doing, the fucking bastards."

Their light turned green, and Langham released the handbrake, moving forward slowly, then with greater speed as the traffic got moving. "Yep. Took Jason out of the city to where the CCTV stopped, then transferred him to a car—all of them outside the barn were Fords, Renaults, or Volkswagens according to Dane. He couldn't make out definite colours, just that they were dark. Adam, even though he used a torch, couldn't remember either. Bit of a shit, that, but we can't force them to recall all the details however much it'd help us. Whoever was driving the van must have continued on through Lower Repton and reentered the city from that end, took the van back into Littleworth's street that has no CCTV, and left it there as though it had never been gone in the first place."

"Apart from the dent."

Langham nodded. "Apart from the dent. Ah, here we are. Wedgewood Road, and number seventy-five is right about...here."

Langham parked, then they both got out. Langham immediately went to the van, fixed in place by a couple of closely parked cars, to give it a once-over. He flashed his pocket torch over the side. The dent was pretty big and deep, as though another large van or similar had smacked into it. Hopefully, they'd get some paint transfer, something to go on so they could locate the driver of the mystery vehicle and find out where the accident had taken place, whether a glimpse of the person driving Mr Littleworth's van had been spotted.

Langham strolled up the path leading to Mr Littleworth's house, a semi-detached that spoke of a hefty mortgage or that Mr Littleworth, if he'd paid the bank off, was a wealthy man. Oliver steeled himself to meet someone like Cordelia Shields, a woman they'd encountered in the Sugar Strands case, all posh toff with a clipped accent and an air of superiority. When the door swung open after Langham had pulled the bell cord, Oliver's expectation was completely dashed. If it was Mr Littleworth standing before them, he was a working man who had grafted hard to get this kind of home, his roots remaining embedded. A white vest covered a protruding belly, a pair of grey tracksuit bottoms bagged on his legs, and his white-sock-encased feet poked out, a hole in each toe. Oliver shifted his gaze upwards. The man had a day or more's worth of stubble, dallying on becoming a beard, and dark semicircles as plump as orange segments hung beneath his eyes.

Yep, he worked hard all right.

"DI Langham, and my associate, Oliver Banks," Langham said, revealing his ID. "Mind if we look at the van before we take your statement?"

"Oh, hello. That was quick. Yep, hang on a sec while I put me slippers on." He moved to walk away then turned back. "Want to come in a minute?"

"No, thanks. We're fine waiting out here."

"Righty-ho."

Mr Littleworth disappeared through a doorway to the left then came back, tartan slippers on and a set of keys in hand. He opened a door beneath the stairs to the right then pulled out a jacket. He shirked into it, the fleece lining looking like it would be warm on his bare arms.

"Come on then." He stepped out and pushed between them. "I'd like to make this quick cos the footy's on in a bit."

Oliver and Langham followed him to the van. Mr Littleworth handed Langham the keys and stayed with Oliver on the tree-lined path. Langham put gloves on, opened the back doors, and peered inside.

"Weird business, this," Mr Littleworth remarked, sniffing. "You don't expect your van to get nicked then put back, do you."

"No. I think you'll find it'll need to be taken away," Oliver said. "Have you got other means of transport?"

Mr Littleworth nodded. Sniffed again. "Yeah, got another couple of vans down the yard, but it's not the point, is it? Pisses me off that someone feels they've got the right to pinch me motor."

"And you didn't see them take it?" Oliver asked.

Langham climbed into the back of the van.

"That's the weird thing, see." Mr Littleworth twitched his nose. "Like, I was awake till late, would have heard the engine start cos it's a noisy fucker. Kind of does this popping thing, gives a bit of a strangled splutter, know what I mean?"

Oliver nodded. "And you didn't hear it?"

"No. Reckon they must have pushed it up the road or something. I did have the thought it must have been someone who knew the van made that noise, but then I told meself I was just being a daft sod and to pack it in."

Oliver went cold, and goosebumps assaulted his skin without warning. The roots of his hair seemed to waver, as though something was telling him that what Mr Littleworth had said was right. Holding a hand up so the man didn't speak again, Oliver walked to the rear of the van and stared inside. Langham crouched by the right-hand-side door, frowning at the spot his torch beam illuminated.

"Mr Littleworth just said something interesting," Oliver said quietly, relating the bit about the car being taken by someone who knew it made strange noises when being started.

"Oh really?" Langham jumped out and closed the doors. "I can't find anything in there. Forensics will have to give it a good going over. I'll have to get uniforms down here for door-to-door, see if any neighbours saw or heard anything." He rang that in, then moved to where Mr Littleworth stood. "I'll need a full list of the people you work with, if that's possible, sir."

"More than possible," Mr Littleworth said. "I can give you names and addresses. I'm the boss, see, so I know where every single one of them lives." He strode towards his path and said over his shoulder, "Come on then. Like I said, the footy's on soon. I don't want to miss Man United giving Arsenal some welly, know what I mean?"

Mr Littleworth had two bald employees, so Oliver and Langham started with them. One was a portly man in his fifties. As Adam or Dane hadn't mentioned any of the men they'd seen as being of the bulky persuasion, and he had the alibi of playing after-hours darts down The Golden Swan off Drummond Road until four-thirty in the morning, they discounted him. The other, a Martin Eggleton, wasn't in at the time they called, but a middle-aged female neighbour kindly, and with much excitement, lost no time in telling them he was a weird sod who came and went at odd hours and ate a lot of Indian takeaways. Oh, and pizza, too, pepperoni—she knew that because once there'd been a circle of meat on the lid when the man in question had tossed the box out onto the path for the recycle collection.

"Reckon he has something to do with it?" Oliver asked as they made their way back to the station so Langham could file a couple of reports. He hoped Eggleton was guilty so they could sort this shit out and get back to normal—normal until the next case, that was.

"Who knows," Langham said on a sigh. "Can't be sure until we speak to him. Get him down the station. If he gets antsy when we ask him to be in a lineup so Adam and Dane can see if they recognise him, we'll be closer to knowing whether he's just a weird git who doesn't like cooking for himself or if he's been up to no good."

"Wonder when he'll turn up?" Oliver licked his lips in anticipation of the hot, if somewhat over-stewed coffee back at the station. It was better than a kick in the teeth, and he needed the caffeine. Looked like it was going to be a long night.

"Time will tell."

They reached the station and went inside, Langham waylaid by another detective on the case. Oliver left him to it, striding down the hall towards Langham's office. He stopped to fill a Styrofoam cup with jet-black coffee along the way. He dumped three sugar cubes in it for good measure—it would take the bitter taste away—and took a seat behind the desk.

He leant back, thankful when his head met the top of the seat, and closed his eyes. It had been a bitch of a day, full of revelations, those revelations coming much faster than the ones in the first murder. The deaths were related, no two ways about it, and he could only hope they managed to wrap this up before a third was committed. Somewhere out there was a gay man, minding his own business, unaware he might already be in the sights of a bunch of bald-headed killers with a mind to chain him up and whip him.

Oliver sighed with frustration. Jason Drum and Thomas Brentworth were keeping what they knew to themselves—or maybe they weren't able to get through to Oliver for some reason or other. Whatever, he wished they could. Wished they'd give him a bit more to go on, otherwise, what was the point in him even being there?

CHAPTER ELEVEN

The call came at two in the morning, jolting Langham away from his office and springing Oliver upright in the chair where he'd been dozing, or 'resting his eyes'.

"Right," Langham said into the receiver, "I'll let them know." He put the phone down then looked at Oliver across the desk. "Got to give Adam and

101

Dane a call later. Martin Eggleton's been picked up. They're bringing him in now. We've got time to question him then set a lineup for first thing. Let's say nine, gives us a chance to let Adam and Dane know they need to take a couple of hours off work. The lads might recognise him."

"*If* he's one of the men." Oliver yawned, groggy from his catnap. He dragged a hand down the side of his face, the feeling that he'd been run over almost taking him for a funny turn. He winced as his stomach churned, the nasty coffee swirling with no hint of coming to rest soon. "I need something to eat." He rose then walked to the office door. "You want anything?"

Langham grinned. "A plate of pie and mash wouldn't go amiss, but seeing as the vending machine only spits out crisps and chocolate, that'll have to do. Thanks." He bent his head and resumed typing.

Oliver left him, walking out into the hallway where the vending machine sat, a rectangular hulk, wide and black, its front glass bowed as though the manufacturers had aimed to make it more attractive. It hadn't worked. Flyers were attached to the sides with sticky tape, telling whoever read them that by calling Crimestoppers you could remain anonymous—they just wanted any information you might have. Another poster announced some officers needing support for a charity event—paragliding, then upon landing they'd be running ten miles—and he used the pencil dangling beside it on a thin, dirty length of string to scribble his name and that he'd pay them ten pounds max if they got to the finish line.

Oliver fed coins into the slot and selected them both a packet of Walkers—cheese and onion for Langham, salt and vinegar for him—and a couple of Snickers. It wasn't ideal, but like Langham had said, it would have to do. They'd work through the night, Langham interviewing Eggleton, Oliver standing behind the two-way glass trying to get a feel for the bloke and waiting for Thomas or Jason to speak. They'd been ominously silent. That happened sometimes, but with Sugar Strands, he'd got used to being contacted quite regularly, and, luckily for them, just when they needed help. This time...well, it looked like they'd be doing a lot of the detective work the old-fashioned way.

He waited for the food to drop into the tray then scooped it out. He nipped into the office to put it on Langham's desk then made his way towards the small kitchen on the other side of the large, main office area. Coppers sat at desks, some bleary-eyed, some bright, as if they'd had a good night's sleep, and Oliver got the very real sense that there was a mission to be accomplished— solving the case before another man got killed. They'd been told about his prediction, that Thomas' death was the first of many if they didn't catch those responsible soon, and with Jason's murder, he'd been proved right.

He went into the kitchen, opening the fridge, not expecting to find the two Cokes he'd stashed there months ago, behind a loaf of bread that, at the time, had been on the turn. The bread was gone, but the Cokes weren't, and he took them out and wondered whether someone had borrowed and replaced them continually until today.

Back in Langham's office, bored and useless to anyone, Oliver munched his crisps and Snickers. Everyone else was busy, and Oliver felt that deep, gut-wrenching sense of being *un*. Unnecessary. Unwanted. Un-bloody-noticed.

He shouldn't be feeling that way, not when the most important thing was preventing death, but how could he help prevent it if he couldn't do something constructive? He opened the spare laptop to do a search on Eggleton, see if he could dig up any dirt that might be useful when Langham interviewed him. Someone had already done this, but Oliver wanted to make sure nothing had been missed.

The man was clean, not even a parking fine. He appeared the model citizen, and Oliver went deep inside himself to test out that new sense of his. He closed his eyes, resting his forehead on his crossed arms on the desk. Relaxing his body, he went into a state where he was aware of everything around him yet was inside his mind, floating, then soaring, flying to the farthest reaches in search of something, anything to give them hope.

An image formed, blurry, so indistinct he couldn't make it out. Frazzled edges appeared, sharpening quickly, rendering the visual into several bald men, naked. A communal hum started, so abruptly Oliver jumped. Was this just a scene from his imagination? After all, he knew about the humming men, knew what would happen next, too, but what if it wasn't what had gone before? What if he was seeing something in the future? He couldn't risk not finding out.

He went with it, waiting for the men to become sharp. Then he moved, mingling with them, leaning towards each one and sensing their breathing, erratic and heavy, their thoughts, '*got to kill, got to kill, got to kill*', their body language, fluid, easy...sure. They were a different breed, people he couldn't understand because they inhabited a place in their minds where only the bad lived. Their bloodlust was up, and he knew without understanding how or why, that their escalation from straight strangulation to strangulation and torture had given them power. A heady, rich sensation, abrupt and blunt took over him—no soft edges here, just pure, unadulterated feeling. These men thought what they were doing was right, just, and wholly what they'd been born to do.

How did you compete with that? How did you explain to them, if they were captured, that what they'd done was wrong when they believed it was so incredibly *right?*

Oliver floated some more, pressing up against a man who he thought might be the leader and letting his essence enter his body. Like rancid, organ-shrivelling poison, evil swarmed through him, infiltrating every part of him, his mind swirling with much more information than he'd thought he'd get.

That evil, that venom, showed him a vision of the next person they planned to kill and where it would be. His blood seemed to freeze to ice, sweat popped out of every pore, and nausea swept up his windpipe until he heaved, raising his forehead from his arms then smacking it back down.

Oliver saw another barn, a tractor parked in one corner and a plough in the other and, standing in the centre, his eyes gaunt, fright etched on his face, was himself.

Eggleton sat opposite Langham at a white Formica table scarred with countless gouges from countless criminals, maybe from a few coppers, too. A coffee or tea stain, a circle the exact size of a Styrofoam cup base, looked worn and faded, the station cleaner probably unable to get the damn thing off.

Oliver eyed him through the two-way glass, aware of a uniformed policeman standing in the shadows by the door, and waited for some telling body language or a vocal slipup that would give them the opening Langham needed to go full pelt into interrogation mode. Eggleton remained normal, so normal Oliver thought they'd picked up the wrong man and it was useless continuing. He'd been wrong in the past, though, so didn't alert Langham in his earpiece that this might be a pointless exercise.

Eggleton had alibis for both murder nights, which were being checked as the scenario in front of Oliver played out. This man would get to go home, maybe with extra weight on his shoulders in the form of huge chips, or maybe with relief that he was in the clear. Either way, Oliver felt this wasn't their man.

But he knew the men responsible, Oliver sensed that keenly. Only Eggleton didn't know it yet. He was helpful, eager to give any and all information, and Oliver decided to try that floating thing again. With no idea whether it would work but vowing to give it a damn good try, he stared at Eggleton's forehead and let everything else fade away. His eyes glazed, and although he was aware of where he stood—in an empty, shit-coloured room—he was no longer there but hanging in time and space, in a limbo land between the waking world and another that was inexplicable and so new to him he only had instincts to rely on, to guide him.

Far from being afraid, Oliver entered Eggleton's head. He was there in spirit, waiting with a scurry of thoughts racing in front of him in the form of hazy lights, the kind caught on camera, car lights, streaks of white and red eels, their tails tapered. Eggleton's mind was full of them, darting, streaking thoughts that pinged against the inside of his skull in his attempt to find something that could be of help.

Questions came from Langham, and the answers zipped in front of Oliver, echoic, ghostly voices that began firm and ended weak.

"Who do you think would have stolen the van?"

"No idea. Everyone I work with is a decent sort as far as I know."

"Who else has a bald head at work?"

"No one except me and that fat bloke...what's his name...? Can't bloody think of it."

"Has anyone given you cause to feel uneasy? By that I mean, has anyone's demeanour changed recently? People acting furtive, jumpy?"

"No, everyone's the same. Except Len, but then his wife's just lost a baby, poor cow, so..."

"Have you encountered anyone who has been talking in a group, or even someone talking on a telephone, and they seem...different?"

"No! There's nothing. I mean, it's not like I go about listening to every Tom, Dick, and Harry's business, is it? I go to work, pick up my van and job list, and get on with it."

"Are you sure you haven't heard anything? Think about it for a second. I'll go and get you a coffee. Or would you prefer tea, water?"

"Tea, milk and two sugars, thanks."

Langham left the room. Oliver waited for Eggleton's thoughts.

Tea. Reminds me of something... The break room earlier. Peter going on about some barn dance. Barn... Coincidence? Yeah, that's all it is. A barn dance they were going to invite some psychic wanker to. They. Who are they? Who else was there? Peter. And that limp-wristed fucker with the dodgy eyebrows. Monobrow. But they've all got hair. What's with this bald shit anyway?

Oliver reversed out of Eggleton's head, returning to his body with a nauseating *whump*. Langham had come back and placed the tea down.

"What did you remember?" he asked.

Oliver wanted to throw up. *Some psychic wanker...*

Eggleton babbled his thoughts, sheepish, apologising for his information, that it was nothing, just a load of bollocks he'd overheard.

"That's for us to decide," Langham said. "If you could remember all who were present, all their names?"

"Peter. Definitely Peter. And the bloke with the eyebrow. Fuck, what's his bloody name?"

Eggleton paused, and Oliver imagined those darting lights, pistoning through his head at speed.

"Chad someone." Eggleton frowned. "No, Brad. That's it, Brad. Don't know his surname, though."

"That isn't a problem. Anyone else?"

"Yeah, but I can't think who they were. I can see them in my head—not much fucking use to you, though, is it?"

"Can you try to recall what else they said? Times, dates?"

Eggleton's frown deepened, and he raised a hand to his chin. He stared to his right at the floor, then looked up to stare at the ceiling. "Tonight. Yep, I remember now because I thought it was weird having a barn dance in the week, what with work and whatever the next day. Shit, I need to ring my boss, tell him I won't be in on time today."

"That will be taken care of. I'll ring him for you."

"Cheers."

"It's me they want to kill," Oliver said.

They waited in an unmarked car in the street running parallel to Mr Littleworth's yard.

The sun was struggling to wake, a blanket of mist pulled up to its chin, and as it peeped over the top, the sky was given a dull iron colour. Mr Littleworth's employees were due into the yard by six to collect their vans and head out to complete the day's electrical work. Littleworth was already in, having been abruptly woken by Langham's call that they were closing in on which employees they needed to question.

"What? Surely you don't know that for certain." Langham tapped his fingers on the steering wheel, peering down the road for cars containing the men they sought.

"I do. Things have...changed. I saw them in my head. As they would have been in the barn and warehouse. I...fuck, this is going to sound nuts again."

Langham waved one hand, imaginary fly swatting. "Go on."

"I went inside one man's head. Saw what they have planned. Saw myself, in another barn."

"Interesting. I still can't get over this shit. Your shit. Not that it's shit, but—"

"I know what you mean, what you're saying. I can't get over it either."

"I can't even begin to imagine wh—"

"You don't want to."

"No." Langham sighed. "So they're calling them barn dances. Sick fucks."

A dark-grey Volkswagen Golf turned into the yard, a snort of exhaust fumes gusting out of the tailpipe.

"Emissions. Should pull him up for that," Langham said.

"Hardly top priority."

"No."

A black Ford Focus followed the Golf.

"Nice motor." Langham stopped tapping.

"I'll go with it," Oliver said.

"Go with what?"

"Whatever these men have planned. Be available when they...get me. You lot can keep tabs. Follow."

"I don't think so."

"But what if they don't show up today?" Oliver swallowed. "What if—"

"Then you stick by my side until we find them."

Oliver mulled over what might be happening inside the office in Littleworth's yard. The beefy man had been instructed not to let anyone leave once they arrived for work, then, when everyone was present, he was to ring Langham's mobile so they could go in. Several more cars and a couple of small vans swerved through the gateway then parked, men spilling out of them and entering the office. Ordinary men, most of them anyway, with a couple of crazies sprinkled in for good measure. But that was life, wasn't it? All right, not everyone

111

had a penchant for killing, but amongst the average were those with a difference, their minds not working the same as everyone else's, and that was what made up the world. Maybe eighty percent normal, twenty percent nuts.

Langham's phone trilled, and he answered. "Right. I see. Let them go, get on with their day. I'll get someone else posted out here." He ended the call and dialled a number. "Langham. Officers needed outside Littleworth's. No, just to sit and watch. Men need sending out to those addresses I left on my desk—might catch the bastards before they get up. Yep. I'll wait here. Let me know when you've brought them in." He nodded, jabbed the END CALL button, then turned to Oliver. "Fucking no-shows. Should have known. Thought they'd have acted as usual, though. Still, we'll get them. Three men calling in to work, all supposedly sick. Not good."

"No." Oliver's stomach rolled over. "Not good at all."

CHAPTER TWELVE

Adam rested his head on the back of the sofa and closed his eyes. It had been a hard day. The long soak he'd had in the bath hadn't done too badly in easing his stretched muscles, but it hadn't completely made the soreness fade away. He felt himself sinking into sleep and welcomed that weird sensation where he floated between awake and oblivion.

"What the fuck?" Nervous laughter. *"Shit, you scared me!"*

Adam was shocked to have Oliver Banks' voice in his head and nearly opened his eyes and sat forward. A sliver of unease crept out of the crevices in his mind. He opened his mouth to call out to Dane who was in the kitchen cooking. The only thing that emerged was a gargle of sound.

A muted scuffle, then the unmistakeable chill of something being wrong filled Adam.

"Mr Banks?" A rush of relief came after he'd spoken, churning with the chill. "That you?" He felt stupid asking when he knew damn well who it was, even more stupid that if Dane came in it would look like he'd been talking to himself.

Minutes passed with no contact.

"Aww, fuck. Adam, you can hear me?"

"Yes! What's happening?"

"I need... You have to get hold of Langham. They've got me."

"Who's got you?"

"The fucking barn men!"

"Oh Jesus. Dane! Dane, come here, quickly."

"What? What's wrong?" Dane asked, hurtling in.

"Mr Banks...he's talking to me. The barn men have got him. Ring the police. That Langham fella."

"What? And say what?"

"Just tell him what I said, for fuck's sake."

Adam closed his eyes. There came the beeps of phone buttons being pressed, the tone an annoying pressure on his nerves.

"I'm in a car. A Golf. Moss green. Number plate starting with W and ending KMP. Number 6, I saw that. Bald men, two in front, one next to me. Going full tilt towards you—Lower Repton. I'll let you know if we go past your place. They're talking about a barn. Won't be the last one they used—police presence still there. Fuck. Coming up to the cottages."

"Our cottage?" Adam gave an almighty heave forward and propelled himself off the sofa.

He opened his eyes and staggered out into the hallway, lurching to the front door, aware of Dane following, phone to his ear, relating what Adam was doing. Adam told him the number plate, the make and colour of the car. He swiped for the door handle, missing several times in his panic before he found purchase, wrapping his fingers around it and turning. He tugged on the door, swinging it open, stumbled out into the night, going down the path. The rumble of a vehicle's approach sounded as he finally made it onto the street, his breaths heaving out of him.

Where the fuck was the police protection when he needed it? Maybe it was shift change, maybe they'd decided protection wasn't needed, but shit, it bloody well was. Why hadn't they been informed that no one would be outside in a car keeping an eye on them? Or had Langham ordered their babysitter to drive in the direction Oliver was coming from in order to waylay them before they got this far?

The green Golf sped past in a blur, no other car following, and Adam raised an arm, waving at it slowly—as if him doing that would make the driver stop. The taillights, two bastard, bright-red rectangular eyes, mocked him, growing smaller, the car creating distance between him and it at startling speed.

"You just went past! Dane, Mr Banks just went past in that car!" His voice sounded like a forty-five on thirty-three rpm, low and distorted, weird as fuck.

"Jesus, they're going too fast. We're going to... Get off me! Let me see!"

"Mr Banks?" Adam slurred.

"I can't see. Blindfold. We're slowing. Taking a right. Ground uneven—car's jostling. Potholes. You got that?"

"You turned right. Onto a track. Potholes. Dane, tell Langham. Tell him."

"Jesus, Adam, you're freaking me the fuck out," Dane said.

"Just do it."

Adam ran down the street. Frustration bubbled inside him, and he tumbled forward, landing on his knees. Pain shot into his legs, and he absently knew his skin would have angry red scrapes when he investigated them later. He got up, legging it, reaching the last cottage in the row then going past it, stepping into the road where the pathway ended. Dane's heavy breathing and stuttered commentating behind him let Adam know he was still on the phone, and he felt calmer for that. Help would be on the way, and knowing this spurred him to focus on the road ahead and pace himself so he didn't burn out before he found Mr Banks.

He judged, from the time lapse between him seeing the Golf and Mr Banks telling him the car had made a turn, that he would be nearing the track soon. But the speed the car had been going— there were two right-hand turns along here. Which one was it? He pushed on, lungs burning, the whip of the cold air freezing his ears. His feet ached already—he wasn't one for exercise—and his thigh muscles protested with the sharp stab of cramp threatening to make his legs useless. A stitch jabbed his left side, and he raised a hand to cover the area, knowing it would do jack shit in easing the pain, the reflex natural.

The first right-hand turn appeared around a slight bend, and he sped across to it—smooth, newly laid asphalt. He took a chance and carried on.

Dane called out, his voice reedy and thin, and Adam didn't need to glance over his shoulder to know he was lagging far behind. The sound of another vehicle broke through the ragged breaths in his head, and the sight of a car coming towards him gave Adam hope at first, which switched to dread when he considered the fact it might be the Golf coming back. He darted into the hedgerow, the ends of branches harsh on his bare arms, scratching. The vehicle glided past, a male driver

117

with a female passenger inside, paying Adam no mind.

Relieved, he came out of the hedges then ran on, a road sign way too far in the distance for his liking. When they drove it didn't seem far at all from Lower Repton to here, but running was a different matter. He remembered the sign read Mereton Marsh and shouted the information back to Dane, not stopping to check if he'd heard or not. Mr Banks being silent was playing on his mind. Had he lost the psychic thread?

"Mr Banks?" he panted out, throat sore from the cold air, his chest tight, a band of strength squeezing. "Can you...can you hear me?"

With no response, Adam battled with the rise of panic spreading through him. He needed to remain focused, not let fear have the upper hand. He trudged on, the road sign seeming to remain far away, and prayed harder than he'd ever prayed before.

CHAPTER THIRTEEN

Oliver was grabbed by the arm and pulled out of the car onto soft ground. It sprang beneath his feet—he'd take a guess at it being grass. He dragged in a deep breath, and the cold air seemed to freeze his lungs. Fear played a factor—he was rigid with it, knowing, because he'd had that vision, that he had a way to go before he got to where he'd seen himself bound and ready for slaughter. Part of him wished they'd just take him there now, get it all over and done with so he didn't have to hold back the piss that threatened to soak his legs. The other part...well, he didn't want to move at all, could do with stalling for as long as he could so help would arrive before anything happened.

He was tugged forward, the grip on his arm hard and relentless, his skin pinched between what he could only imagine was a finger and thumb. Whoever had hold of him took pleasure in squeezing, and he bit back the urge to call them wankers for giving him sharp, nipping zaps of pain. He stumbled, righting himself quickly while counting his footsteps. He reached only seven, then the ground changed to a harder substance, and if they'd taken him to a barn like he'd thought, then he imagined he stood on concrete surrounding the structure. There were no pebbles, nothing to tell him what else it could be.

A deep wail of sound penetrated his ears, the vibrations unnerving and sinister. Door hinges bemoaning being used. Someone prodded him in the back. He lurched forward, flailing his free arm to brace himself if he fell, but managed to remain on both feet. The air changed, the scent of it, less the freshness of outdoors and more the interior of a stable.

Bumps crackled under his shoes—hay, had to be—and he was released, the disappearance of that hold a small mercy. His skin throbbed as if the biting fingers were still there, and he imagined bruises would leave their ugly, plum-coloured marks by morning.

Would he be alive to see them, or would Hank be the one examining them while Oliver lay cold on the slab? Hank, who could determine that those bruises would have been made while Oliver was still alive.

That thought gave him extra chills, standing alone more so, in a place he couldn't see. The loss of his sight had been anticipated—Thomas and Jason had been treated to the same, hadn't they. He'd fallen into the trap of trusting someone he knew, even though that person had crept up on him while he'd been standing outside the station taking a breath of fresh air, waiting for Langham to finish work so he'd get a lift home. And who would suspect an abduction outside a cop shop anyway? Who would be so brazen as to walk over and bundle you into a van with the risk of being spotted by a member of the force?

He listened for signs of what would happen next, although he knew. If they played this one the same as they had the others, he'd be stripped naked soon, told to do as they asked and placed centre stage. That humming would begin. Once that started, his time was limited. Adam and Dane had said the hum had gone on for maybe five minutes until the whipping.

Oliver surmised he had about half an hour of living left.

That sobered him further.

Something coarse—rope?—brushed his hand. He shivered, wincing by instinct in case they decided they were going to hit him. No blow came, nothing but the prickly awareness that they stood close, watching him, gearing themselves up for the treat to come. And it *was* a treat to them, the highlight of their lives maybe.

His arms were wrenched backwards, wrists held together by the itchy material. His ankles were bound, too, scuppering any chance he might have at escaping. He was a little off balance, and he concentrated on getting used to standing with his feet so close together.

"Stay," a man said, his voice deep and chilling and calm. "Stay."

It sobered him yet again, and he forced himself to make his body and mind relax.

Silence loitered around him—maybe the men had gone off to get undressed and discuss the final plans on how they'd kill him, who the fuck knew—but the air held an edge of expectancy. It sizzled around him, menacing, too *there* for his liking. He ignored it and concentrated on a speck of white, twinkling light in the distance, like the spiky pattern of a hand-held sparkler on bonfire night. It grew in width as he stared, and he wondered if it was the heart of his new gift, the energy he needed to tap in to in order to see the future or reach out to speak to people like Adam.

"Adam?"

His voice lacked strength; it wouldn't have got through. He projected information to Adam instead, reminding himself of what he'd told the young man. The number plate. The make and colour of the car. Where it had headed. It struck him then that even though there was meant to still be a police presence at the other barn, there couldn't have been. It was so close to this one, albeit on the other side of the road and maybe half a mile away, but if Adam had passed on the information, Oliver should be hearing sirens about now—or, if the police had decided against audio announcing their presence, at least the *crack-snap-crack* of tyres outside and the hum of car engines.

There was nothing but the sound of his breathing and the beating of his heart.

"Adam!"

In his mind, free and unshackled there, he ran towards the sparkle of light until it was as tall as he was, all serrated, writhing sparks with a circle of intense whiteness at its centre. Heat came off it, not too hot but enough to warm his face, and energy rustled in the air between him and the light. He inhaled it, the burn travelling into his lungs, and the heat went to work there, too, expanding, growing in strength until his cheeks blazed and he buzzed with other-worldly power. He was as hot as he'd been when finding Thomas Brentworth strung up on that red metal girder.

"Adam! What's happening? Is anyone on their way?"

The pant of heavy breathing came, and it took a second or two for him to realise it wasn't himself or the men but Adam.

"Yes! Dane's...following... Got a few hundred feet to... Soon..."

Oliver filled in the blanks, relief scouring through him, and he relaxed his muscles a bit, smoothing the edge off the pain in his shoulders and neck that had been growing steadily since he'd been taken out of the vehicle. A snap of sound to his left had him tensing again, though, and the full force of the pain came hurtling back, only stronger, with more venom. If he could just get through the next few minutes he'd be saved. Providing Adam had taken the correct turn.

"Can you see the barn, Adam?"

The shuffle of feet.

"Adam!"

Hot breath fanned his cheek, sour-smelling, alcohol-laced. That was a revelation. Neither Adam nor Dane had mentioned the fact that the men had seemed drunk, just that they'd had glazed eyes.

"Adam! Can you see the fucking barn?" The hairs on the back of Oliver's neck stood at attention. *"Please say you can fucking hear me, Adam. Can you see—"*

"Yes! I see it. Up on a rise. A car—several cars— some light coming through, maybe a doorway?"

A tug to his T-shirt hem and the sound of material slicing had Oliver's stomach rolling over, but he held firm, half in this world, half in the other, holding on to that invisible ribbon that bound him to Adam. It could fray at any time. His T-shirt was removed, and the cold steel of scissor blades skirted up his legs, his jeans and boxers cut away. The cold attacked his skin immediately, and he shivered, conscious of his cock dangling, free for them to inspect.

"Argh!"

That word from Adam was accompanied by the sound of bumps and scuffles, much like listening to someone dropping the phone while you waited for them to pick it up again and resume your conversation.

"Aww, shit, Banks. Fucking hell, no."

Oliver's heart raced—what had happened to Adam? Had a man posted outside spotted him? He tried to call out in his mind, but being roughly manoeuvred into a kneeling position took all his attention, the sparkle of light growing smaller, flashing less brightly, his focus shifted to the now. He strove to keep the faint light in his mind—so long as it flickered even a little, if he could still hear Adam, he'd feel less alone.

"My ankle! There's a bloody ditch all around this place. I didn't see it—grass is so long. I'm in the fucking ditch!"

Oliver almost asked aloud where Dane was but stopped himself. He thought it instead, pushing the words towards the light, hoping they reached Adam.

"Dane's coming, Oliver. I see him entering the field from the road now."

"How long will he be? Did he see you fall? What if he goes down in the ditch, too?"

"I don't know if he saw me. He's... Police shouldn't be long. I'm...I'm looking over the edge of and can see headlights. Maybe five minutes away."

"Five minutes? Shit."

If the men followed the same pattern, Oliver was safe, but if they upped their game, changed their plans, five minutes was plenty enough to kill someone.

The humming began, and Oliver would never have thought he'd be so pleased to hear it. They were going ahead with their weird ritual, and by the time they finished humming and whipping, the police would be there.

They couldn't arrive soon enough.

Adam closed his eyes in an attempt to ignore the pain streaking through his ankle, but it didn't work. He opened them and leant his back against the side of the ditch, which was a head shorter than him. Dane came nearer, growing bigger with each step, but he wasn't as close as Adam wanted him to be. He needed to get his attention so he didn't take a tumble into the ditch, too. If they both ended up in there, ankles broken—he was sure his was—they ran the risk of Mr Banks being killed.

He hadn't thought much beyond getting there, finding where Mr Banks had been taken, and now he had a chance to think about it, there wasn't an awful lot he could have done had he made it to the barn. Yeah, he could have burst inside, interrupted the proceedings, but with so many men as the enemy, Adam didn't stand a chance against them. They could overpower him easily, add him to their victim list, trussing him up like that poor bastard in the other barn.

Dane was within hearing distance now, and, keeping his voice low, Adam called out a warning Dane slowed, trod carefully, and came to a panting stop, the toes of his shoes close to Adam's nose. Dane bent over, peering down, hands on knees, his legs slightly bent.

"What the fuck?" Dane asked breathily, bunching his eyes closed and baring his teeth. "What are you…doing down there?"

"I fucking fell. Think I broke my ankle." As though hearing him, Adam's ankle throbbed harder, and a lance of pain ricocheted through the bone then spread into his shin, up his thigh, and attacked his hip. "Oh Jesus, that hurts. Did you tell the police where we are?" He needed to make sure, to hear it.

"Yeah, estimated time of arrival"—Dane stood straight to lift his wrist and click on the light so he could read the time—"about four minutes."

"Fuck, that might be too long. Will you go?"

"What, in there? In the *barn?*"

"Yes!" Adam frowned. "Or if you can't, help me out of here so I can go in."

"It isn't safe. Us going in there isn't going to be of any help. Not if—"

"But what if they haven't got that far yet? What if they're only doing that ritual shit at the moment? We can't leave Mr Banks. We can make a noise. Distract them." Adam paused to wait for an answer. It didn't come. "Right?"

"I don't know. We saw the state of the last bloke they killed. We know what they can do. We shouldn't just stand by and let that copper be killed, but... It isn't as cut and dried as that, is it? *We* could get killed as well. I'm shitting myself here. Fucking *shitting* myself."

"Help me out." Adam held up one arm, gritting his teeth at a fresh bout of pain.

Dane hauled him up, and Adam hopped on his good leg to get a safe distance from the ditch. He gingerly lowered the other foot, grimacing, another sharp-as-hell pain shooting from his ankle right up his shin bone, exploding into splintered pinpoints in his knee.

"It's broken. Damn it to fucking hell and back." He ground his teeth, and despite the raging agony, managed to hop-hobble to the track he should have been walking on in the first place. He took Dane's offered arm for support.

"We can't go in there, Adam. You'll be no good the way you are. One whack from them, and you'll go down like a sack of shit."

Adam nodded. "I know, but I just... I just want to help him. I was left in that alley. No one knew I was there. I was left and I don't want to leave him."

A caterpillar of cars turned onto the track, stopping halfway to the barn for officers to tumble out, running on silent feet towards them. Langham led the way, and as he drew closer, the panic on his face was stark in the moonlight. He raced past,

the other officers close behind, and they flooded
through the barn doorway and disappeared inside.

Oliver heard the arrival of new people, heralded
by shouts of "Get down! Get down on the floor—
now!"

His legs weakened even though he was
kneeling, the humming mercifully gone now,
replaced with scuffling feet, yelled protests, and
police orders. Arms encircled him, and he flinched,
panic rising over who had taken hold and dragged
him along. What if one of the men had grabbed
him with a view to using him as a hostage? What if
he got killed anyway, regardless of the police
being there?

"It's all right, it's me," Langham said.

He pressed Oliver's shoulders until he sat on
something cold and hard, then removed the
blindfold. Oliver's first sight was Langham's face,
his anxiety plain in the furrowed brow and
grimacing mouth.

"You all right?" Langham asked, going to work
on untying the rope around Oliver's ankles. "As
well as you can be?"

Oliver nodded. "Yeah, just cold."

"Someone get a damn blanket!" Langham
roared, turning to look at the activity behind him.

Oliver stared, too, taking in the scene of naked
men on their bellies, wrists cuffed behind their
backs, faces in the hay, their heads shining from
the torch beams, sinister and just plain odd.

Officers hauled some to their feet and marched them outside. The killers were all bald, and it reminded Oliver of something.

"Where's Littleworth?" he asked, scanning the people.

"No idea, why?" Langham freed Oliver's wrists.

"He's the one who took me."

"What the fuck?" Langham's eyes darted from side to side, his mind clearly working overtime.

"He's the one who got me outside the station. Put me in his van then dropped me off to the other three in the Golf."

"Jesus fucking Christ, that sneaky, pissing wanker!" Langham took his mobile from his pocket and jabbed a few buttons. "Get someone out to Littleworth's house and yard—now!"

CHAPTER FOURTEEN

Adam woke on the sofa, wondering what the hell the time was. They'd returned home in the early hours after he'd been seen to at the hospital and they'd given more statements to the police. Sam had been understanding about them not being able to go into work, and seeing as it was another of his barns that had been used for the previous night's 'dance', he had other things on his mind.

The image of knee-high piles of pig shit came to mind, and he felt for Dane having to shift that lot tomorrow. Adam wouldn't be able to work for a few weeks—not until the cast came off his ankle—but his time off wouldn't leave them too short of money. Sam had graciously agreed to give sick pay. Adam had felt more than grateful about that. He didn't look forward to the day when he went in for another X-ray, though. If his bones hadn't knitted together, he would have an operation in his future. Little metal plates would be inserted, the bones screwed to them.

Switching his mind back to Sam, Adam smiled. He'd mentioned Adam and Dane as being "The best shit-shifters I've ever had, and I'm not wanting to lose you in a hurry."

Dimming light seeped through the gap in the curtains, and he guessed it must be after four o'clock in the afternoon. That was about the time it got dark these days, and with the rumble of his stomach came the scent of some stew or other, no doubt a tasty concoction Dane had made. He sat up and swung his legs over the side of the sofa, easing his casted foot into the ugly shoe the hospital had provided, all black plastic sole and blue Velcro straps. Whatever painkillers they'd prescribed had deadened the pain so he could fall asleep easily, but the faint promise of it returning nagged in his toes and shin.

He stood then reached for the crutches propped against the sofa arm and gripped the handles. He needed a piss, a drink, and food, in that order. As he lurched into the hallway, Dane came to the kitchen door and eyed him with a look of concern.

"Everything all right?" he asked, worrying a black-and-white-checked tea towel in his hands.

"Yeah." Adam smiled. "Yeah, I'm doing okay. Dinner smells good."

"Old biddy over the road dropped it in. Heard about what happened, thought we might need feeding."

"Of course she did." Adam smiled again. "Doubt there's much she doesn't hear about."

"You need some help?" Dane nodded at the crutches.

"Nope. Thanks. I can manage." Much as Adam wouldn't mind Dane to lean on rather than the crutches, he had to do this by himself.

"All right. Well, I'll just be cooking the potatoes to go with this casserole. Mash or boiled?"

CHAPTER FIFTEEN

*PSYCHIC STAYS AS POLICE AIDE—BUT HE ALREADY
KNEW HE WOULD!*

*Psychic police aide, Oliver Banks, has admitted, a
month after his involvement in the Queer Rites case,
that said case almost had him putting his skills
aside and trying to lead a normal life.*

Banks, apparently contacted by the dead and led to their murder sites, has been a police aide for some time now. He's known for helping with several one-off murders and the more well-known Sugar Strands and Queer Rites cases. Working alongside Detective Langham, Banks has proved himself a valuable asset to the city police. Although some people have scoffed at his ability, it might be folly to assume it's all a load of hogwash. Time and again his information, relayed to him from fresh corpses, has been a vital part of catching those responsible for their deaths.

However, the Queer Rites case took a sinister turn when the killers targeted Banks as their third victim, blindfolded and taken to a remote barn on the outskirts of sleepy Mereton Marsh. If it wasn't for Banks' special ability in being able to communicate with a civilian helper through thought—can you believe that?—he would undoubtedly have been killed.

Why the victims were killed hasn't become evident. None of the twenty-three men responsible are offering any explanation. The mastermind behind the operations, a Mr Littleworth, has also declined to give police any answers. The men are being held in Stratford prison while they await trial.

Banks, minutes from the same fate as the previous victims, was able to get help by sending his thoughts to a man named Adam Parks of Lower Repton. When we asked Banks how he felt about his experience, he declined to elaborate fully, but he did say, "I've thought about giving this up, but if I stopped helping the police I'd be going against everything that is good. People may not believe I do what I do, but that's neither here nor there, is it? I hear the calls and I relate the information. As long as the dead speak, or the living project thoughts and words to me, I'll be here to listen."

Whether Banks' claims to hear the dead are true or not, we applaud him in his dedication to helping fight crime. With the state of our city, we...

Oliver stopped reading and scrunched the front page of the newspaper into a ball. The use of 'apparently' by the journalist with regard to him hearing the dead pissed him off, but there was nothing he could do about it now. His editor boss had listened avidly as Oliver had told him as much information as he'd been allowed and reminded him that now the Queer Rites case was basically over, he ought to get himself into the office kitchen and make a round of teas. Make himself bloody useful.

He sighed, home now after a long day spent making those rounds of teas and fending off the editor, who had kept pushing for more than Oliver was comfortable giving. He reckoned he'd have to find another job for the times in between helping the police, because the money the force paid him now didn't equate to anything he wanted to shout about, nor could he afford to live solely on that. It was a token gesture, the pay of an informant, really, and he'd never get rich on it no matter how many times he helped out. Working at the newspaper had seemed like a Godsend at the time he'd landed the job, but his boss was becoming increasingly insistent on prodding for information, and Oliver was uncomfortable with it.

Still, if he stayed, he might always feel this way about being the local rag's tea-making boy. Returning to that kind of work after the thrill—and fright—of accompanying Langham on a case was a huge letdown. No adrenaline flowed, the hours dragged by, and he had the sense he accomplished nothing at all. Unless he counted slaking people's thirsts as the highlight of his day.

THREE MONTHS LATER

Oliver was drifting to sleep, belly full, his heart content.

He thought of tomorrow and wondered how many rounds of tea he'd have to make. Today had been twenty-three, with two coffees thrown in for good measure, and Cheryl from reception had even had the cheek to ask him to nip to the local Tesco and get her a carton of orange juice. It had got him out of the office, but fucking hell, he wasn't employed to stand in a queue behind several other people—mostly mothers with red-faced, yowling children in the trolley seats—wishing he was anywhere but there.

The tick of the clock faded away. Blackness crowded at the edges of his mind, growing as it crept towards the centre of the supermarket scene in his mind, and sleep would embrace him soon.

"You didn't find me."

The male voice, such a *quiet* whisper, almost went unnoticed, but the hairs on the back of Oliver's neck stood on end, goosebumps streaking from there to cover his skin. The air chilled. He snapped his eyes open, pushed up on one elbow, peering over to check the time. Eleven o'clock. He'd been lying there an hour, then, waiting for sleep to come. It hadn't seemed that long. Had he drifted off without realising it, the voice coming to him in a dream?

"Hello?"

No, it hadn't. The voice was louder this time, still a whisper but one full of urgency and pleading. The harshness of it brought more goosebumps, chilled the air even more, and he had the horrible thought that this spirit might not be a good one. Oliver sat up.

"Are you there?"

Yes, he was there, but he had the unnerving question of whether the voice was from someone alive or dead. Since he'd been able to communicate with Adam, he now didn't have any clue—they sounded the same.

"Can you hear me?"

Oliver nodded—stupid, really, if it was a living person, because they wouldn't be able to see him. He got out of bed and went into the living room, heading for the kitchen on the other side.

"Yep, I hear you." He picked up the kettle to check how much water was in it. There was enough for him to have a cuppa, so he switched it on. "Who are you?" He took a cup off the mug tree and spooned coffee and sugar into it.

"Simon. I'm Simon."

"Alive or dead?" Blunt, but Oliver was tired, and he needed to know.

"Um, dead?"

"Okay, where are you? I don't mean whether you're here with me, either. Where is your body?"

"Warehouse."

"Aww, fuck. That case is closed. All the men involved were arrested months ago. Is that you, Jason? Thomas?"

"I know the case is closed. But you didn't find me. I've been...waiting. But after the foxes found me, bit my feet and legs... There isn't much of me left, and while there's still a bit, I want my parents to have something to bury. You can still see it's me. Kind of."

"Oh Jesus. All right, um..." The images he conjured in his mind weren't pretty—a man with the skin gnawed off his body, bones protruding, a rope of intestines dangling from a lower belly that had been sliced open with sharp claws. Unsure whether he'd thought that up himself or whether he was being shown, he swiped the visuals away. Took milk from the fridge and made his coffee. "What's left of you?"

"Hair. Skin. I watched myself bloating then shrinking, and loads of stuff came out."

"Fucking hell." Oliver swallowed down bile. "Right. I get the picture. So, do you know which warehouse it is?"

"No, but I know what it looks like."

Oliver sighed inwardly and took a sip of coffee. Burnt his tongue. Not knowing where the warehouse was would prove a pain in the arse if this bloke didn't give him some decent landmarks to go on. He could only hope he would.

"It's bright orange."

Oliver knew the location immediately. The warehouse, an oblong metal behemoth, sat on top of a hill behind the retail park off Gainsborough Avenue. It had been used in the past as a place for people to store their shit, for a price, but the company had gone bust several months ago. It now stood empty, a huge, white hanging tarpaulin FOR SALE sign on the front, red letters visible from the road when he waited at the lights—those bloody, seemingly never-changing lights—to turn into the retail park.

"I know it. We'll be there soon."

"You will?"

"Yep, we will."

"I couldn't get through before. I tried, but it was too hard, and then the others came, and they said you were the one to speak to, and I tried again. Every day I tried, and tonight was going to be my last time and..."

"Don't worry. You'll be able to move on now."

"Yes, but...God, I can't even tell you what's bothering me. You'll see when you get there."

"What? What's bothering you?"

"It doesn't matter. It's vanity. Shouldn't be letting it affect me now, not when it isn't important. I'm not there, am I? I'm...here. Somewhere else. That body isn't...me."

Oliver waited for more, blowing on his coffee then drinking. There was hardly a rush if Simon had been there a while, was there? Still, a sense of urgency gripped him suddenly.

He went upstairs and rang Langham.

"Morning already?" Langham said.

"No. Someone spoke to me."

"Aww, shit. Fuck's sake!"

"Someone from Queer Rites."

"What?"

"Not a new one. Don't worry, they haven't got a second group doing that shit."

"Thank fuck," Langham said. "Who is it? Where?"

Oliver dressed one-handed. "Some bloke called Simon. He's in that orange place off Gainsborough Avenue."

"The old storage warehouse? They were pushing their luck using that."

"Doesn't look like they did, does it? Simon hasn't been found—if he was, we'd have known about it."

"True, but you'd have thought... I know the place went bust, but you'd think people would have visited it to buy it. Prime place for business, that."

"Obviously not." Clothed now, Oliver strode towards the bathroom. "Are you going to shift your arse out of bed so we can get there?"

"Yeah, yeah, give me five more minutes. I need to call it in anyway. Besides, it's not like we don't know who put him there, is it?"

Those bastard lights refused to change again, no one in front of them waiting to turn into the retail park, and no one behind. Yet the red light remained, staring down at them like a strange, knowing eye. Oliver sighed, trying to hold in his irritation. There was no rush this time, but a sense of getting there fast for the spirit's sake had got hold of Oliver. What if them finding Simon was the only way he could move on? What if, now the killers had been apprehended, this was the last link for Simon, the last thin thread keeping him here? Oliver wanted to help the man let go.

Langham turned onto Gainsborough Avenue, ignoring the turnoff to the left for the retail park, and climbed the steep hill road where the orange warehouse sat. Oliver stared at the monstrosity, its colour rendered a dull, rusty red with the moonlight shining behind it. The rear of the flat roof had treetops peeking over. A car park was at the back, he knew that as though he'd been up here before, enough space for a hundred or so cars. A forest spread out from its far edge, where the foxes lived, no doubt.

As they drew closer, Oliver made out the blue streaks of light from the roofs of other officers' cars, cutting intermittent swatches in the darkness, bringing the bright orange of the warehouse front into view. There was a second or two where it seemed as though the whole world had held its breath before sighing, a signal that everyone could proceed. Langham steered left and parked beside two police cars there, switching off the engine and taking a deep inhalation.

"Ready?" he asked, tapping his fingers on the steering wheel.

"Not really. Never am, but not to worry." Oliver got out, his legs heavy, his body weary but his mind fully alert. He closed the door, the sound a slam in the eerie quiet. He followed Langham to four uniformed officers standing outside, a set of their car headlights casting them in a white glow.

"We waited for you, sir," one of them said, a blond, six-foot-or-so man with a thin moustache that looked like it couldn't quite make up its mind whether to grow thicker or not.

"Right." Langham went to a set of glass doors. "Anyone find out who owns this place?" he called back.

"Yes," a black-haired officer said, "but they're on holiday."

"You checked for other entrances?" he asked.

"Yes, sir. One at the back. Padlocked roller door. Some windows up top, too high to get to without a ladder."

"Anyone got a rammer in their boot?"

"Yes, sir," Officer Blond said.

"On you go then." Langham nodded to him. "Break the glass." He walked back to Oliver, took booties out, and handed over a pair. He put his on. Then came the gloves. "How the fuck did they get in if the back's padlocked?"

Oliver shrugged, covering his boots. "Maybe they broke it then put another on there?"

"But what about an alarm?" Langham toyed with his chin.

"Might not have one. I'd say it's empty. Nothing to steal."

"Yeah, but still. There's an opportunity for vandalism. Squatters. The owner isn't bothered about that?" He shook his head. "Makes you wonder, doesn't it. Owner supposedly goes bust, is skint, then fucks off on holiday?"

"You think the owner could be involved?"

"No idea. Needs looking into, though."

Two stout barks of sound, then the shattering of glass further twanged Oliver's nerves. No alarm went off—that answered one question—and Officer Blond propped the rammer against the wall then reached inside to open the door. It must have been kept secure with a simple knob mechanism that turned and clicked the lock into place, because the door opened when Blond pushed it inwards. Maybe the owner locked those doors from the inside and left the building via the rear roller. There was no keyhole here.

Langham went to his car and opened the boot, returning to Oliver with two torches. He handed

145

one over to him. "Just in case the electricity's been switched off."

As it happened, it hadn't. Blond was inside and had turned on the lights.

"Right." Langham motioned for Blond to come out. "This is just a search for a body, nothing else. You find it, you call out. Don't touch. Watch where you step for scene contamination purposes."

The four officers nodded and disappeared inside, booties and gloves on. Langham and Oliver followed. The reception area had cream-painted walls and a plain teak desk with one ratty grey chair behind it. A dirty, white-painted door to the rear probably led to a staff room or toilet.

"We'll check through there later," Langham said. "May as well search the main part first."

Through double opaque plastic doors, the kind that swung and slapped shut in hospitals, was a long corridor with separate storage rooms to their right. Each space was divided by a wall, every one of the doors open, suspended like knobbly metal rolls of carpet at the top. The storage rooms didn't reach the ceiling. They walked along, peering inside each one. At the end, another hallway stretched to the rear, and more rows of rooms and aisles in between started to their right. Oliver imagined that from above it would resemble supermarket aisles, except here the goods weren't on show. Down the second aisle, the four officers went in and out of the rooms.

"May as well make a start on the third row," he said.

Langham nodded, shouting for the uniforms to take row four next, and every even row after that while Oliver and he took the odds.

It wasn't until aisle nine that Oliver felt weird. The hairs on his arms rose, those on the back of his neck quickly following, and his mouth dried. His skin prickled painfully, as though someone stabbed him with a million pins at once. "Down here," he said, tugging Langham's arm.

He led him three doorways down and saw, in his mind, the image of a young man standing at the rear of a room, twenty or so naked men in front of him, preventing any escape. Jam-packed, they were, only the bodies of the first row visible, the rest just a sea of shiny heads. The men hummed, the sound of their unified noise filling the small space, an angry swarm of wasps ousted from their nest. All those men versus one... Even if Simon hadn't been blindfolded with his wrists tied, he hadn't stood a chance.

"They forced him in here," Oliver said and jerked his head at the room beside them.

"So where the hell is he?" Langham stared into the room for a while then went in.

Oliver remained in the doorway. "I don't know. I saw him in my head, in this room, with them doing that humming shit, but after that..."

"Concentrate!" Langham said, looking over his shoulder.

"I have been!" Oliver closed his eyes and shut out the sound of Langham pacing. "Simon? Are you here? Can you help me to find you?"

147

No answer.

The image of a body, chained to another form of pole, filled his mind. He got an impression of stairs and immediately darted to the end of the aisle, calling out to Langham, "Quickly. Over here." He followed his senses, rushing to the rear of the warehouse where a set of metal stairs rose to a veranda that appeared to have no use whatsoever. Had it been used as a lookout at some point, the owner keeping tabs on customers in the car park during busier times? Oliver took the steps two at a time, his boots clanking on them, then stood on the veranda, staring out over the warehouse.

Langham joined him.

"There's nothing but room tops and aisles," Oliver said.

"What?" Langham frowned. "Of course there isn't. What did you expect? Simon to be sprawled out on top of one of them?"

Oliver peered down at the officers still checking the rooms. They reminded him of ants, busy, intent on their mission, probably secretly hoping they were the ones to find Simon, yet at the same time hoping they weren't.

"Where the fuck are you, Simon?" Oliver said quietly.

"Behind you."

Oliver swivelled. A row of windows. "I don't see you."

"That's because you're in the wrong place."

"What? You said the orange warehouse." His words echoed.

Langham rolled his eyes and shook his head, muttering something about useless information and a waste of police time, not to mention disturbing his sleep. Oliver let the testiness slide.

"Yes, I was there, but I'm not there now."

"I can bloody see that! Where are you?"

"Foxes? Think about it..."

"Fuck," Oliver whispered. "He's out the back."

"The back?" Langham leant towards one of the windows in the row and stared out into the darkness.

"Shit, I think I see him," Oliver said.

"Where?" Langham squinted.

"Not out there, it's too dark. I see him in my head. They chained him to a tree."

ONE WEEK LATER

"I still can't get over finding Simon like that." Oliver slid Langham a baguette across the desk.

"Like what? Is it because you're used to seeing the corpses fresh?" Langham pulled the clear wrap off and took a healthy bite. Mayo sat in one corner of his mouth, but he licked it away.

"Yeah, there is that, but I meant him having no cock." Oliver winced at the memory.

Langham swallowed, pointing at his food as if to say the conversation wasn't ideal at the moment. "Um, yeah, that was rather nasty."

"Still..." Oliver opened his own food. "At least it was ripped off *after* death, eh?"

"Bloody awful," Langham said.

"Bloody foxes."

"Indeed."

They ate for a minute or so in silence, the visuals in Oliver's head souring the taste of his food. He pushed the images aside and thought about what they had to do next. Langham still had the final bits of paperwork on Simon to file, then they could go home.

"Excuse me? Can I trouble you for a second..."

"Oh, fuck me..." Oliver raised his hand so Langham didn't speak. "Yes, love, carry on." He waited for the female to speak again, wondering what the bloody hell was about to come their way now.

"It's just that I'm in this flat and I can't get out."

"Um... Are you alive?"

"I have no idea. I just know I'm in this flat, and every time I think I'm dead, I wake up again."

"Where is this flat?"

"See, that's the thing. Again, I have no idea..."

Oliver looked at Langham and smiled apologetically.

"Fuck it," Langham said. "You put me off my bloody lunch talking about men's cocks being torn off anyway. What's next? Lay it on me."

Printed in Great Britain
by Amazon